Vignettes en Route

Vignettes
en Route

Jajabor

Translated from the Bengali original *Drishtipaat*
by
Alokojjal Banerjee

NIYOGI
BOOKS

This English edition is courtesy New Age Publishers (P) Ltd., who are the publishers of the Original Bengali novel *Drishtipaat*.

Published by

NIYOGI BOOKS

D-78, Okhla Industrial Area, Phase-I
New Delhi-110 020, INDIA
Tel: 91-11-26816301, 49327000
Fax: 91-11-26810483, 26813830
email: niyogibooks@gmail.com
website: www.niyogibooks.com

Design: Shashi Bhushan/Niyogi Books

ISBN: 978-93-81523-04-9
Year of Publication: 2012

Printed at: Niyogi Offset Pvt. Ltd., New Delhi, India

To my revered parents,
Piyush Kanti and Kalyani,
who are no more,
who bore with them a whiff of the times
gone with the 'Vignettes en route'

Collator's Submission

This work needs an introduction.

A Bengali youth went to London in 1936 to study law. When the Indian boarding house at Gower Street was ravaged by German bombings during the Second World War, he was persuaded by his well-meaning relatives to return to India. On the eve of the arrival of the Cripps Mission at Delhi, a provincial newspaper in England engaged him as their special correspondent to cover the event. He used to contribute occasionally to that paper during his stay in London.

From Delhi, the youth wrote a few letters to a female friend. This piece is collated from those letters. Save the very personal and familial issues of the correspondent and the recipient, nothing has been deleted from the letters; although certain changes have been inevitable in names and places for the sake of confidentiality.

The literary talent displayed in these brief missives bode the possibility of developing further, through wider penmanship, into deep maturity, later in life. It is a matter of grave lament, that his premature death in an accident some years ago has pulled the curtain finally over that possibility.

One

We touched ground at the Willingdon airport after seven hours of air travel. Although not large, this airport has its strategic importance. As war broke out in the eastern hemisphere, this airport became the main base of entry and exit for various British, American and Chinese military experts.

Our carrier was a twin-engine Douglas. Avian ancestry ranks it immediately after the Flying Fortress and the Liberator. Though not a pure blood, it would still rank among the nobles. Huge in bulk, it roars mightily and moves at lightning speed.

The mythical stories of the Puranas tell us about the flying chariot, Pushpak, which ferried men to the heaven. The final destinations of modern aeroplanes are located on earth, but a lack of skill on the part of the charioteer (the pilot) may land its passengers at heaven's door any moment.

The chief officer of the aerodrome hails from Bengal. The gentleman is young in years and of an affable disposition. His wife Monica Mitra's renowned beauty is the cause of bitter pangs in the hearts of many a Bengali woman of New Delhi.

One descends from the airliner via a flight of wooden stairs. A strange feeling of wonder infuses the being. Only this morning I was in Calcutta! On the way to Dum Dum airport, when not all the gaslights had been extinguished. On the footpath, the Hindustani shopkeepers were still sleeping under wraps on their charpoys. The Oriya coolies of Calcutta Corporation were rushing, hosepipes in hand, to remove the wastes accumulated on the well-trodden paths of the city, with Ganges water. Hawkers were making rounds from door to door on their bicycles, the day's newspapers heaped on the handles.

A trace of slumber from the just-bygone night still lingered on the earth. A crescent moon of the dark phase shone lacklustre, atop distant rows of trees, resembling the pale visage of a sick siren. A few dying stars still glimmered faintly in the sky. Only nesting birds on roadside trees had woken up with a flutter of their wings. The tall chimneys of jute mills far from Dum Dum airport looked like an indistinct painting on the canvas of the sky. Clad in spotless white uniforms, white-skinned employees of the airline were busy checking tickets and weighing luggage. In the distance, along the road to Barasat, bullock carts were trailing in a long line; a feeble cacophony from their oil-starved wheels renting the air.

It would be New Delhi as the clock struck one-thirty. There was an hour-long intermission at Bamrauli for breakfast. Had one made such an arrangement, one could leave Delhi after lunch, return to Calcutta and catch a movie at the Metro. By train it would take a day and a half. Glory be to science which has brought the far, near and has made the inaccessible, easily accessible!

I remember my childhood. During long afternoons, the men would be away at their workplaces. Mother would lie down in the adjacent room, the ends of her sari spread out on the floor, a novel by Bankim in hand—a befitting siesta avocation after the mid-day meal. Guarding her short-lived resting hour against noisy interference by the restless child, the grandmother sat engaged with the grandson. Fixing her nickel-plated spectacles over her dim vision, the old woman read out verses from the *Ramayana* in a low tone. Tired of tossing and turning and fussing with the pillow, suddenly the boy's ears would catch the refrain,

'Ravana rides the Pushpak chariot with flair,
Gaining the speed of lightning in the air!'

Hooked for more, he followed the route of the chariot that flew across forests, mountains, seas and dales, like a migratory bird, from far to farther, from one country to another. The idle mid-day hours became fired up with the single-minded imaginings of a child. The sheer fortune of ten-headed Ravana infused such envy in him! Not for his hundred thousand sons and even more grandsons, but for this adroit ability of being airborne at freewill.

That old grandmother has long left this world, together with her devotion, beliefs and prejudices. She could possibly never have imagined that her grandsons and granddaughters would rival the great overlord of Lanka in a not-so-distant future. I can't recall if Krittibas, the poet who rendered the *Ramayana* in Bengali, had mentioned how long the son of Nikasa took to reach the golden isle of Lanka, but the aerial distance of nine hundred and three miles between Calcutta and Delhi was covered in seven hours by us. There is, in it, a lot of excitement but it falls short in evoking pleasure. This is, sort of, popping Vitamin C pills instead of savouring juicy oranges.

In the pre-aeroplane era, traversing the distance was not the sole motive of journeying; a length of time was then available for building up ties of relationship en route. Leave alone the era of slow-moving bullock carts, what travelling by rail offered by way of journeymen's camaraderie, air travel completely nullified. Post-war India will definitely see an increasing rise in civil aviation. Having boarded a plane at 9:00 pm from Dum Dum airport, after dinner at the Great Eastern, one might sit for breakfast, following a good night's sleep in the air, at the Taj in Bombay. Then, neither the trouble of buying a ticket on the might of blows or bribes, nor altercations with the porters and the fracas of co-passengers, will be the order of the day.

Nobody will then arouse sleeping passengers in the middle of the night with a loud call near the window, '*Chagram*' (Hot tea)! No longer will there be watermen to fill the cupped hands of weary and thirsty travellers, or pointsmen to pass trains by, waving green flags from their tin-roofed signal towers. Modern technology has lavished upon mankind speed, but has forced out emotions. The pleasure of motion is there aplenty but the leisure of rest—not a bit!

No transport was available outside the aerodrome. My watch indicated it was one-thirty in the afternoon. The scorching March sky wore a pale colour and the air was thick with dust. The asphalt road lay ahead, nearly empty. Vast fallow-land lay on all sides—east, west, north, south, upwards and downwards—whichever way the eyes travelled, the senses were impressed with the feeling of a scalding exhalation of hot air. I had read Tagore's poetry on the fierce and unkind weather of late April (*Baisakh)*; but the real import of the lines, 'Voracious leaping flames of a pyre, licking the vast skies', bore meaning to me for the first time here, on this summer mid-day in Delhi. Seven of my co-passengers were foreigners. Their military fatigues bore signs of the class they belonged to. They departed in accompaniment of their luggage, in a big tarpaulin covered motor truck.

My destination was uncertain as I had not booked a hotel room. In this unknown place, my only repositories of trust were my feet. I reckoned whether to hit the road with those.

'Where to? May I offer you a lift?'

Was it an illusion? They say ghastly sirens beckon only at night; do they call out even during the day? No, I turned and found Mr A.S. Bokhari, my only civilian co-passenger in the flight, the Fuehrer of All India Radio, standing by his vehicle with its open doors. I was so carried away by the offer of a ride at this cul-de-sac in the scorching mid-day hour, that I'm sure if the best danseuse of heaven had prostrated herself before me, I'd not have been happier.

The world of media speaks both ill and well of Bokhari sahib in equal measure, although his approbation in the government circle has helped him gain promotions—from one zenith to another—till he became the chief of the All India Radio. He was a professor in Lahore University before that. He'd earned wide acclaim in Urdu literature through his sarcastic essays written under a pseudonym. His repartees and gags are wonderful! Lionel Philden imported him to the world of radio from the world of learning. He is akin to Sisir Bhaduri of Bengal, in his transition from the lecture-room to the studio.

Not only him, his brother Z.A. Bokhari had also built a cushy nest within All India Radio, through the good offices of Mr Philden. No wonder, at one time the All India Radio was nicknamed Indian BBC–Bokhari Brothers Corporation.

The streets of New Delhi are pleasing to the eye: straight, wide and shady; even and smooth, bitumen-covered, not slippery or overflowing with the contents of vats and dustbins. A limited number of vehicles ply the streets, so they are safe for the pedestrians. Ever-foraging, fearless herds of buffaloes do not stray or litter on the streets, unlike in other Indian towns and the chances of being spat upon one's head with chewed betel juice from the inside of a roadside house, does not exist. There are small circular parks all over, from where roads spike out in all directions like spokes in a bicycle wheel. They call these parks 'place', but it's the same everywhere. Windsor Place differs from York Place by name alone. It is built with care and is maintained with care!

The identities of streets are bureaucratic in nature. The names of many former British employees in the Government are engraved in shining letters by the streetside. The importance of the name of Chief Commissioner Bailey here far exceeds the name of Babur, the Mughal Emperor. That is why Baird Road is more posh than Noorjehan Lane. One thing is clear; the Councillors of New Delhi would not earn notoriety on account of an outsized humility. I must mention in this connection that one road here has been named after Rabindranath Tagore, during his life time, something that is not yet a reality in the poet's birthplace. Familiarity breeds indifference.

Mr Bokhari dropped me off at a place named the Queensway. A good name indeed; it instantly reminded me of its Bengali equivalent–Raneerdighi. I decided to leave alone the matter of digging in the morphology of names, as I badly needed to address several pain-inflicting factors of my body—hunger, thirst and fatigue.

The urgency in war preparations has multiplied the number of government offices extraordinarily fast. Almost all the houses and lodges of the city are filled to capacity with clerks, record keepers, officers and employees of the government. A good many well-paid government officers of the Secretariat are living in tents in the open field! Droves of newspaper reporters have arrived from all over the globe. All the hotels and boarding houses have put 'No room' signs on their reception desks. I failed to secure a place of stay for myself, even after seven days' continuous efforts and agreeing to pay a lofty price. Tagore had written, 'I longed for many days, to dwell in a corner of this world, immersed in the play of my mind, caring not for wealth, nor for honour, but only for a small nesting place.' I guess the poet must have been to Delhi sometime.

The man who helped me with generous hospitality is the local chief of a private company. He has put the company on good footing through his skilled efforts. The city of New Delhi was built to serve the government; the sticker on its forehead reads-'On His Majesty's Service'. If Jamshedpur has the sobriquet Steel Town, then the sobriquet for New Delhi should be Steelframes Town! The population of the city has grown pivoted around the Secretariat. In this peon, record-keeper, clerk and superintendent-infested city, non-government persons find it very difficult to be noticed. Here, the source of honour and influence lies in the pages of the *Indian Gazette*. Those few non-government persons here, who have managed to establish themselves in a society lorded over by the secretaries and the joint secretaries, truly deserve reverence. My host, Mr Sen, is the President of the local Emergency Relief Society, Secretary of the Kalibari, an Executive in the Bengali club and a distinguished member in many other organisations.

Rows of bound volumes of *Sabujpatra*, a respectable Bengali literary magazine, in the wall-cabinet, testify to his taste. It became more evident at mealtimes. Only typical Bengali everyday items featured in the menu. A bitter appetiser, fries, dal, vegetables, fish curry, a sour side-dish of sorts, a little curd. No ostentation for a guest. Tiffin in the afternoon was also simple but decent; fried flaked rice with a garnish of coconut or a few home-made white *puri*s. The artificial sumptuousness of sweetmeat from the confectioner's at teatime and the abundance of a European bill of fare at lunch or dinner was not there as a reminder to the guest that he was only a visitor. To make one feel at home and at ease speaks of culture; pompous display smacks of conceit. That conceit might be borne of wealth, learning or power.

Two

Once Shree Radha, the heroine of Vaishnava verses, had lamented in great agony for the exiled Lord Krishna, 'My indoors are outdoors and the outdoors are my indoors.' Surely one cannot afford to confuse Connaught Place of Delhi for the flower-filled bylanes of Vrindavan, the backdrop of Vaishnava verses and of course, none of the ladies of town for daughters of Vrisabhanu, the mystic father of Shree Radha. But the fairer sex here have indeed, on summer nights, made the indoors, outdoors and outdoors, indoors.

Of course, they have no choice either. All through the day, the sun god Lord Martand shines so fiercely here that the inner quarters of the houses heat up like the fire-bellied boilers of Tata Steel Company. Any attempt to rest indoors ends up in frustration. The rotating blades of the fan blow out only hot currents of air. Consequently, sleeping outdoors is the only option.

It's not women alone, young and old of all ages have a similar experience and assemble outside. In the evening, pots of water are poured on the grounds adjacent to the house to help the earth dissipate some heat. Charpoys are placed on the ground to serve as beds. It gives the impression of a ward in a government hospital. Spouses, parents- and sisters-in-law, siblings and children all share the same unbarred space under the open sky. Neither is there a cover overhead, nor curtains around the bed. To unaccustomed eyes this might seem a bit awkward.

Like other standard customs and moral principles across the world, one's sense of decency is also relative. Social mores and the nature of the land introduces variations; necessities initiate modifications as well. One might see a Marwari woman walking non-chalantly on the streets of Barabazar in Calcutta, dressed in a short blouse and an eighteen yard long ghaghra that leaves uncovered much of the ample torso in between. None of our Bengali ladies would take a fancy to a dress like that. English and Anglo-Indian girls move freely, clad in short skirts that end well above the knees. It is never an eye sore. Yet, none of our ultra-modern, adventurous society girls would dare lift the length of her semi-transparent crepe sari from the standard ankle-length up to her knees. Even if one gives it a try, no one would be able to look at her out of sheer embarrassment!

How identical items appear decent or indecent due to the differences of association, language and ambience, becomes very apparent in the case of movies. I have observed that those who sit through scenes of long kisses and intimate embraces of Greta Garbo and Charles Boyer unhesitatingly at the Metro, even if accompanied by senior in-laws or younger members of the family like the daughter-in-law, son-in-law and daughter, feel awkward as the romantic scenes of the hero and the heroine unfurl in a Bengali movie even though they have less fire and passion. In a discussion on physiology, the terms which one feels tongue-tied with to mention in public in the mother tongue, may be eloquently used in English while arguing with the same group.

In a land where sleeping indoors in summers causes heat fever, it is natural for men and women alike to sleep outdoors in one and the same courtyard, irrespective of relational ties like father-in-law, son-in-law, mother and daughter, as it is impossible for most of the people to keep more than one courtyard in their houses. New Delhi is a metropolis, a cosmopolitan city. An assembly of people have converged here from all over Anga, Banga, Kalinga, Kashi, Kanchi and Koshal. Even though their individual food habits have not been compromised, uniformity rules their mode of sleeping. The outfits of Punjabi women are especially suited to such community sleeping. The pyjamas, close-fit at the heels, leaves no chance of being dishevelled on the person's body unawares in sleep like a loosely fastened sari does.

On waking up from sleep in the morning, what caught my attention first was the cavalcade of vendors. One gets milk, vegetables, fish, meat and everything else right at the doorstep. Commodities arrive on bicycles instead of being carried on the head by customary seller-women. There are bicycles everywhere. We see only newspaper hawkers on bicycles in Calcutta. Here, in New Delhi, the milkman, washerman, barber, fisherman, butcher, blouse-piece seller, toilet-soap seller, one and all, arrives on a bicycle with a large cane basket or box on the carrier. Merchants of this city are not pedestrian in practice.

The one I beheld at dawn sells milk. Resembling the skinny and under-fed horse of a hackney-carriage, the skeletal remains of the bicycle had a couple of tubs of milk fastened on both sides of the carrier at the back. The tubs are made of tin, fitted with a tap at the bottom which lets out milk at the turn of a knob. A pair of similar containers also hangs from the handles in the front. These two-wheeled chariots have a strange power to carry load and move speedily at the same time. Stranger is the choral symphony of its wheels, chain and the hanging milk-pots clanging together. The covers of the tin tubs are under lock and key. It goes without saying that this serves the purpose of assuring people about the purity of the milk and the reliability of the milkman. It is similar to an unmindful man writing his name onto an umbrella with great fanfare! To get pure milk, without any water, one will have to boil down five seers to two seers.

Following the milkman, came the fish-vendor with his slogans, *'Kalkatta-ka hilsa lo, Karachi-ka chingri'* (Come, buy the hilsa from Calcutta, prawns from Karachi). In most cases, the hilsa may have originated from Allahabad and not from Bengal. But, as in the case of most people, their look is deceptive and only their taste reveals their origins. The basket at the carrier of the fish-vendor's bicycle has a cover of fine net to prevent flies from flocking the wares.

Greengrocers come, one by one. Some cry out, '*lauki lo*' (buy the gourd) and another advertises his '*palang*' (spinach), or '*gobi*' (cauliflower). Some others have tomatoes, '*bhindi*' (ladies fingers), '*hara dhania*' (green coriander) and '*seetaphal*' (pumpkins) in their baskets. Seeing the mountain of washed clothes on the carrier of the washer-man's bicycle, Hanuman himself might have been amazed.

Women's hair and men's beards both require tending and they take time in equal measure. The only difference is that the nurture of the first concerns its growing while the nurture of the second is related to its mowing. One has to tie and dress the hair everyday, as well as shave facial hair everyday. It is undeniable that she, who cooks also finds time to care for her hair and he, who attends office makes time to manoeuvre the razor. Still, getting a helping hand from the sister-in-law in braiding her hair pleases a woman; a man feels relieved to get the help of a barber as he shaves or grooms his beard. Thus, barbers begin their rounds from door to door from eight in the morning. They carry a tiny portable brass heater which looks like an Icmic Cooker. It constantly warms up water on winter days. Residents of cold places know that a slap is more welcome than a splash of cold water on the cheek when the temperature runs below thirty-seven degree fahrenheit in December.

The march towards offices starts at half past nine. At first, it is the run of the attendants. They are turbaned, clad in khaki uniforms, with three or four rounds of red serpentine cummerbund around the waist. A few of them carry in their cummerbunds a small knife with ivory handles inside ornamented sheaths. A mimicry of the castrated guards of the Mughal empire. Those are the attendants to the secretaries or the hon'ble members. They are the major-generals among the ranks of the orderlies. A bundle of files wrapped in a red coarse packaging sits on the carrier of their bicycles, which the sahibs carry home on Saturdays and most of which are returned untouched on Mondays.

The clerks, the assistants and the superintendents follow the march of the attendants.

Bicycles, bicycles and bicycles. They move one after the other as though in a procession. With this are interspersed *tonga*s. That, also, is a two-wheeler of sorts. Pulled by a horse, it accommodates four seats back to back. A snatch of canvas covers the head, but it is too small to really protect against the falling rain or the beaming sun. While boarding and alighting from it, men are tested for their skills in gymnastics and sari-clad women, in their ability to maintain decency. A little lapse of attention may cause a fall or a fainting.

The pace of a *tonga* is slow, the seats are without comfort and the surroundings are offensive to the nose. Recently, the fare has risen by the grace of the Americans. The stretch which was previously charged at four annas is now charged at minimum twelve annas and any attempt to negotiate the amount would invite avoidable adverse comments from the *tongawala*. Better still, one finds co-passengers on the way to and from the Secretariat around 10:00 am and 5:00 pm. The *tongawala* cries out, '*Daftar-ko*! *Daftar janewala aaiye*' (Bound for the office! Come, come office-goers). This divides the fare and makes it bearable for the pocket. The proverb goes that the shared mother of many sons dies uncared for, but, luckily, shared *tonga*s reach the destination anyway.

By half past ten, the adult male population of the entire city is out on the streets. All roads lead to the Secretariat. The babus have made their getaway; commotion settles down and all is at rest; its time for the harried housewife to take a breather.

The Imperial Secretariat is newly built. Not only the Secretariat, the houses and quarters, roads and streets, shops and markets, all are new here. New Delhi as a city is an upstart; it is not tradition-bound like Benaras or Prayag, not even like Calcutta or Murshidabad. It is more like the neo-rich war contractor than a zamindar with an ancestry of seven generations. But this is the era of parvenus. Now, more adorable is a Baby Austin than a horse-carriage, a muff-chain than a seven-stringed necklace, a ghazal rather than a khayal. Amassing wealth suffices now, why bother if it lacks that richness?

Through the middle, up to the iron gate of the Viceroy's house, runs a wide path, the Kingsway. On either side of the path are the two wings of the Secretariat—the North Block and the South Block. Forms, colours, lines and structures of the two are identical, as though a pair of *sandesh* in a sweetshop which are cast in an identical mould. At the head of the flight of steps of the North Block are inscribed on a stone the names of the planner, Edward Lutyens and his assistant, Sir Herbert Baker.

Almost all the government and private buildings of New Delhi mimic largely, though not in its entirety, classical, i.e. Greek architecture. Mostly columns and domes are used; arches are sparse. Those, too, are Romanesque in fashion, semicircular not Islamic, with pointed ends. Columns are round, rather than quadrangular. It is difficult to fathom if any motive worked behind adopting Greek architecture in the establishment of New Delhi. Some believe that the climate of North India approximates Greece, although in Greece, the summer is relatively bearable and the winter is harsher. As in northern India, the air is dry, the sky is clear and the sun shines unsullied over Greece. So, it's no wonder that the architects of the city might have believed that the adoption of Grecian architecture would count in favour of durability within New Delhi too.

But, it would not be just to give any particular definition to the architecture of New Delhi. It is classical indeed, but not orthodox.

The influence of the Hindu architectural style is also apparent in the columns of the portico of the Secretariat which is built after the fashion of the Ashokan pillar of Sarnath. So the ornamentation is with figurines of elephants, bells, etc. at the main entrance and other places of the Secretariat. Alongside, there are stone filigrees which are peculiar to Islamic architecture and so extensively used in the mausoleum of Salim Chisti at Fatehpur Sikhri. Most of the masons who worked here came from Agra, Jaipur and other places of Rajputana. It is believed that many of them were descendants of the builders of the Taj Mahal. Atop both the North and the South Blocks are large domes, nearly resembling the dome over St. Paul's Cathedral in Rome, although an effort was made to impart an impression of Islamic architecture in it. Eyes fail to gather that the height of the domes is only a hundred feet less than the Qutub. In the two Blocks together, there are nearly one thousand rooms and corridors of approximately eight miles in length. It's really grand, no doubt!

Normally, there does not exist much of a relation between government offices and art. Its name evokes in our mind an image of bundled files, fat registers, miscellaneous deeds and accounts. Wherein the sole work involves dealing with heaps of files on tables from 10:00 am to 5:00 pm, we hardly bother about the architecture and environment of the office building. It never occurs to us what the colours of the windows are or how the staircases have been fashioned. We do not expect to see a fresco of an Ajanta painting on the wall of a police court. But, wouldn't we have felt happy to see it, had it been there? I am delighted to see the attempts made to render beautiful at least the Secretariat in New Delhi.

It is a massive building made of red stone. A long path that stretches far runs through the middle. Green grass carpets the ample fields on either side. Rows of fountains in occasionally placed artificial lakes sprout water incessantly. Flanking it are well-tended beds of seasonal flowers—blooming daisies, pansies, asters and hollyhocks. Single orange trees are placed at selected sites. The branches are carefully trimmed to give a round shape and lend the look of an erect open umbrella.

An effort to make the insides of the courtyard not only utilitarian but also visually interesting is evident. Ceilings and walls of the large rooms in the North and South Blocks, known as Committee Rooms, are adorned with paintings of the artists from the Bombay School of Art. The subjects of the paintings are good but are wanting in artistic skills. These large rooms host conferences and meetings of various committees. The first press conference of Sir Stafford Cripps was held in the committee room of the South Block.

Cripps's flight landed in Delhi much later than the scheduled time of arrival.[1] It was two in the afternoon then. So, convening a press conference at four, only within two hours of arrival, was expressive of a man of much alacrity. Most of the South Block is under the military's control, the sole civilian department there is the Home Department, tucked away in a lone corner. The nearness of positions might have been caused by the likeness in the rules of business of the two departments. In India, the police and the military are as close to each other as can be; if not of the same clan, certainly of the same genus.

The army guards the entrance. Entry passes for the reporters and the journalists have been arranged by the Information Department.

Despite my best efforts to motivate the *tongawala* by offering much in the way of tips and even more insinuation to speed up, it was only a few minutes to 4:00 pm when I reached the entrance of the South Block. The poor *tongawala* gave his best. But horses that draw the *tonga*s resemble the indifferent, dispassionate and unattached yogis of India; nothing can really excite them. Speeding is almost impossible.

I rushed to the conference room. Sir Frederick Puckle, the head of the Department of Information, stood waiting with his officials at the head of the stairs. Responding to a familiar face, he said that he was there to receive Cripps. A couple of steps ahead of me was a Caucasian gentleman, who seemed like a reporter just arrived from the UK or US. He suddenly took a few steps back and questioned Sir Frederick, 'Did you say Cripps? That's me'.

A bolt of lightning was perhaps the preferred choice in such a circumstance. We stood amazed; Puckle, at his wit's end, his retinues, stunned.

Sir Stafford Cripps was a member of the War Cabinet. He had arrived to determine the fate of India with proposals from the cabinet of the British Government. He had been put up in the Viceroy's palace. Therefore, it was expected that he would arrive at the press conference in the Viceroy's decorated vehicle, adorned with the Crown, led by a pilot sergeant on a red motorcycle, accompanied by the Private Secretary of the Viceroy, or someone of a similar high rank, to guide him on the way; the grandeur and the splendour would be the unmistakable identifier. It was the common perception. Where was the private secretary or the pistol-at-the-holster police sergeants guarding him at front and back? He came, accompanied by a solitary attendant from the Viceroy's house; indeed, that too was perhaps only to show him the way.

Putting aside all formalities, rules and norms of the government, Cripps created an environment which was easy and simple. India placed greater trust in his sincerity, her people wished him success in his efforts and his reputation was reported with resplendent praise in the newspaper editorials of every language in every province.

Cripps appealed to the members of the press attending the conference to not concoct imaginary accounts of Cripps' proposals or indeed, analyse them too much yet to avoid a sense of resentment or resistance in political circles from fanciful reporting in the newspapers even before actual discussions with the political leadership were held. Obviously, the appeal was the necessity of the hour.

Most surprising was Cripps' unwavering faith in the eventual destiny of his proposals. Cripps had not even an iota of doubt that the agreements reached regarding the proposals, which had been unanimously accepted by the War Cabinet, would be acceptable to the Indian Nationalists hands down, help remove the enmity between Britain and India and be a perfect sequel to the centuries of untold sacrifices and inhuman sufferings of countless freedom-seeking Indians.

The attitude of Prime Minister Churchill towards India was not unknown. Cripps' sympathy towards the aspirations of a nationalist India and especially, his warm cordiality with the top leadership of the Congress were as well known. Among imperialists, Churchill was the most orthodox. Among the socialists, Cripps was the most progressive. A reporter questioned, how the Prime Minister and Sir Stafford had managed to agree while crafting the unanimously accepted proposals? Was it Churchill who had discarded his orthodoxy or, could it be, that Sir Stafford Cripps had changed since?

Cripps replied amidst roars of laughter that it was neither and that a new, hitherto unnoticed, way out was discovered, which eventually became acceptable to both.

The clock struck six when we came out of the conference room. Ruddy rays of the setting sun fell on the reddish wall of the Secretariat building. Water sprouts from the fountains, lying ahead, swivelled outward and into a circular stone well. One could see the war memorial at the far end of the lean and straight Kingsway, on the body of which are inscribed memorials to the Indian soldiers killed in the Great War. From a distance, ruins of the old rock fortress of Indraprastha seemed, like an old, grey-haired, grandmother, long past her prime, beside her young and beautiful grand-daughter, to remind the present-day grandeur of New Delhi of the incontrovertible dictum of time and the irresistible consequence which lies in waiting.

I looked around and saw the Union Jack, the traditional victory sign of British imperialism, fluttering a little in the breeze at the top of the large dome over the Viceroy's house. It has been residing in India for almost two-hundred years now—unmoved, firm and irrevocable. The conference which ended just now had an implicit assurance of change of colour of that flag. Whether it would be saffron or green, or it would have a crescent moon or a wheel with spokes, would be a pertinent question later. For the time being the important thing is that it will be new and Indian. But, when, oh when will that day come, when?

Three

Reba, the seven-year old daughter of the house-mistress, came in and asked me very seriously, 'Minisahib, who will win, the English or the Japanese?'

There is a history in the evolution of the name Minisahib; not only history, but also linguistics.

When we travel to UK, the first mutation occurs in our outfits and then, in our names. Those known in the native country as Poltu, Gadai, Suren or Subodh, become introduced in foreigns land as Sen, Ray, Mitter or Banerjee. New Delhi is not unalloyed UK, but an ersatz one. Here, the identities of people are located, not in their first names, but in the last. Nobody really cares what the first two letters of P.L. Asthana stand for,the last part often suffices. The vocative to be used in addressing a person depends on his status. If he is a clerk, the suffix to be used with Asthana is 'babu'; if an officer, the prefix would be 'Mister'.

But forms of expression change by word of mouth; changes occur in names as well. Often, the deviant forms of names currently in vogue originated in the illiterate pronunciations of servants, orderlies or peons, rendering it very difficult to guess the actual form. Banerjee becomes 'Benarasi', Mister McCarthys becomes 'Markautti-sahib'. Bilasia, the house-maid of the Sens, hailed from the vale of the Ramgiri Hills. Her language concocts a bit of the Dravidian with the Aryan and her manner of speaking is devastating. I am reduced to 'Minisahib' in her dialect. How this occurred, through what deviations and mixes of half-words, exploring that would require help from a languge expert like Suniti Chatterjee.

'Do tell me Minisahib, who will win? The English or the Japanese?' insisted the questioner.

The question is not new. I have been asked this question by many on a number of occasions. Although usually I hardly have to attempt an answer as in most cases the questioner himself provided the answer; what they expected was only a nod in support. Those who refrained from providing the answer, they, too, had not been left in any doubt about their preferred stance, much like the way a wife in new clothes asks her husband how she is looking. Similarly, I returned the question, 'You tell me, who will win?'

'The English!' her tone was solemn and firm. Churchill himself would not have been able to answer with so much conviction.

But opposition was close by. No sooner did the sister's answer reach his ears than the brother ran in. 'What did you say? The English will win? Bogus! Will the English match the Japanese? Pooh!' He added appropriate gestures to his words. Pursing his lips, he assumed an air of such serious slighting that any hope in favour of an English win by his audience was worthy to be regarded as sheer ridiculous foolishness.

Booddhu is elder to Reba by only two years. But the stream of guardianship does not match the ratio of age. Particularly, given that Booddhu attends school and Reba still waits her turn to be admitted. So, in the middle of an argument, when Booddhu draws the reference of his teacher or other fellow students, Reba feels compelled to fall silent. 'Bishu is the first boy of our class. He says so. Do you know more than he knows?' All arguments fail before this.

But today, the aired opinion is not that of the first boy. This is purely his own belief. Reba is not the one to be cowed down. 'Why can't they win? Certainly they'll win!' But her voice lacked firmness.

Booddhu replied, expressing tremendous disdain, 'The English cannot beat the Germans and you think, they can fight the Japanese! They will suffer all-round defeat.'

'Why will they suffer defeat? The English have so many guns, cannons, aeroplanes. Do the Japanese have aeroplanes?'

'What makes you think the Japanese have no aeroplanes? Ha! Ha! Ha! Who sunk the English Navy's the *Repulse* and the *Prince of Wales* by bombing from the air? Could the English retaliate against the Japanese? All the aeroplanes of the English are rundown and broken, what can be done with those?'

'Are the aeroplanes of the English all broken and damaged, Minisahib? If broken, then how do they manage to rise to the sky and fly?' The well-wisher of the English appealed sadly.

But Booddhu joins in before my reply, 'It flies and falls off! Didn't the newspapers write about the air crash yesterday? An aeroplane crashed in Calcutta as soon as it took off. Some people were killed too.'

It's a proof that cannot be disputed. Not only the event, it came with chapter and verse, the precise date and venue. After this, offering further arguments against the premise was difficult. Yet, as a last try Reba protested feebly, 'The English can't be defeated, you will see.'

'You really know it all! They will lose, they will lose, they will lose. The Japanese will capture Churchill and will lasso him, chain his hands and feet before slitting his throat with a razor.' Saying this, Booddhu exited as though he, not the Japanese, were about to arrange for the capture of Churchill.

On the verge of tears, Reba said, 'Never. The Japanese will never be able to do that. Will they, Minisahib?'

I drew her near and said tenderly, 'No, they will not. Well, if they can, what does it matter? Let them lasso Churchill; they can't touch our Reba darling, can they?'

'What will happen to Bill if the English are defeated? They will capture his father, mother, John, Lucy, Annie–all of them?'Bill was their neighbour William. John was the twelve year old son of the Simms couple, the next-door neighbours. Lucy and Annie were his two sisters.

'Well, let them capture them. The other day, their pet tabby had almost bitten our maid Bilasia! No?'

Reba vigorously nodded her head to express her disapproval. She said, 'No, they mustn't be taken. Bill gives me chocolate and toffee. He has assured me that he will let me ride his bicycle.'

Good God! At long last the truth behind this intense goodwill for the British held by our friend of Britain becomes clear. After this, even imagining the defeat of the British could be sheer thanklessness. Really, there is not much to wonder about it. The same holds true for those few Indians who are English afficionados in the country. It may not be chocolates or toffees, but it is rooted either in their service, promotion, or in receiving titles like Rai Saheb, Khan Bahadur, or CIE Knighthood.

But all discussions over the far Eastern war front were interrupted. Ghose saheb and his wife appeared all of a sudden. I was introduced to this pair only a few days ago. But through their endearing qualities we have become close in a short span. Mrs Ghosh proposed, 'Let's go to Okhla.'

'Where is that? Peru or Kamschatka!'

'It's a bit closer than that; on the way to Mathura, only eight miles from here. On the way back, we will take you to Nizamuddin for a visit.'

Okhla resembles an island. The water-stream of the Yamuna has been diverted through a canal there. The canal surrounds a piece of land. The place is shady and full of trees. On one side is the office of the Public Irrigation Department, the remaining part is an amusement park. There is a lock gate to open and close the water source of the canal. A wide causeway covers it. *Tonga* and motorcars can pass through easily. On holidays, people gather here for picnicking. Okhla is the botanical gardens of New Delhi.

The place is pleasing. Amidst grey, rough and dust on all four sides, this place offers an oasis of cool greenery. There is a long dyke to extend the shallow stream of Yamuna water towards the canal. Overflowing the dyke, white water streams fall on the other side. The place is overlaid with stones. The children of the local peasants are busy fishing there with bits of clothes as fishing net. A few sahibs keep vigil for hours with their fishing rods at the headwater of the canal. Their patience is profound and hope unbound. The Seths, the Prasads and the Guptajis have spread their mattresses under the shades of the trees. In all probability, they are the owners of large stocks of irons in godowns at the Chowrie Bazar and all through the week they have earned much money by selling it in tons. Now they have come on an excursion, accompanied by oversize housewife-madams, half a dozen sons and daughters, about four extra-large tiffin-carriers, water pitchers, smoking pipes and servants.

Also there were khaki-clad English, Canadian and Australian army captains, brass-epaulette-on-shoulders in place. Hanging onto their arms are half-caste girlfriends, cameras slung from their shoulder with long leather straps. The onlookers feel embarassed at their exhibition of amorousness in broad daylight.

I have not observed the English behaving so outrageously in their homeland. I have seen lovers in Piccadilly on Saturday afternoons. Their conduct there likens pigeons getting cosy on high treetops. Their merriment, although not in accordance with strict convent rules, obeys an invisible unwritten rule. It's not about morality but decency. The English pay homage to decency in their hearts. The most insulting name-calling in England is 'indecent'.

This sense of decency is not evident across the Channel, only twenty-six miles apart, in the Continent. The youths there flout the ruling finger of decency with impunity.

The English, who had sailed seven seas to reach this country, are completely oblivious of the existence of that line of decency. Stories by Somerset Maugham are replete with notorious anecdotes of the spoils of the Britons outside Britain. In *Travels at Palamou*, Sanjib Chunder wrote at one place, 'Wild beasts are beautiful in the wilderness; babies are so in their mothers' laps.' All doubts in Darwin's theory are dispelled by observing the Britons outside the wilderness called Britain.

The main reason behind the unabashed impertinence of the English in India is that they do not count the bystanders around them as human beings at all. They do not care a fig what we think of them. Nor do they have the responsibility of behaving themselves with us. There is one more reason, something that goes deeper. The English here are totally alienated from their society and families. They are like horses not reined in. They are comparable to the scion of a rich landlord from the countryside boarding in a men's boarding house in Calcutta, with no guardian to put a check on his activities and plenty of dispensable cash in hand.

A pair of English couples has come on bicycle from New Delhi, unfazed by this extreme summer. They came only to take a bath in the river. Water in the river is only chest-deep, but transparent. In there, they swam; or rather, they attempted to swim, with vigour, for several hours. On the other bank, a flock of herons that were silently waiting for a catch by the river, still and focussed, lost their calm at the sonorous playfulness and mirth of the swimmers. Startled, they kept shifting from one spot to another.

Mixed bathing of this kind is not aesthetically appealing in our country. Leave alone old-timers, even those ladies who are staunch followers of the English in manners and customs, do not feel at ease with the idea. Even she who does not feel shy to waltz in a club with other men, after taking a shot of gin or vermouth, does not think very favourably of the idea of mixed-bathing.

Analysing deeply brings forth the understanding that at the root of this is our inherent culture. But by arguments alone, one cannot overcome the pulls of deep-seated culture, like one cannot overcome the fear of ghosts by using intelligence alone. To remove inherent culture overnight needs revolution and to eliminate it in a leisurely manner, requires practice.

In our traditional societal construct, a unified role of men and women is not very distinctly recognised. Their areas are apart, milieus are different and duties are separate. Besides observing religious rituals together, our Shastras have no other mention of joint acts. Other than the section on Subhadra as Arjun's charioteer, there is not a second reference of a joint act by a wife and a husband in our entire corpus of the Puranas, the Kavyas and literatures. Savitri followed Satyaban not to collect twigs together but out of her fear of the evil foreboding she had from a bad dream. In olden times, menfolk were busy in administering, priesthood, teaching, cultivation or commerce. Women were in charge of hospitality of the cow herds and the Brahmins, performing culinary tasks and housekeeping. Time and opportunity of meeting each other were limited and often confined only to the space and time of the bedroom at night.

Our joint family system, too, has obstructed at each step the building up of an all-encompassing and strong bond between the wife and the husband. There the husband and the wife are only the nuts and bolts of a large family machine, not a self-content and unified whole made up of only the two. They are the two separate strains of a melody; not a symphony of the duo. A married woman in a typical Indian family feels hesitant to go out only with her husband, to a movie or for a stroll on the Strand, leaving at home her married and unmarried sisters-in-law. The eldest brother of the family would not dream of an excursion to Darjeeling or Simla with his wife alone.

The idea of a unified existence of man and woman is only nascent in our tradition-bound society. Even after appreciating the separate entities of man and woman, we have only just been able to comprehend a composite view of conjugal existence thanks to knowledge acquired from Europe. Even now, a division of labour between men going outdoors to earn a living and women keeping house is most common. Although the responsibilities differ, there exists now a link that connects these spheres of activity. Women of this era are aware of the world their husbands inhabit.

Home is now no longer built only on the needs of wives or for that matter on what they are at ease with. The world outside is also, no longer, under the exclusive control of husbands whether in choosing male friends, socialising or entertaining. Like prehistoric mammoths, joint-families are now on the way to gradual extinction. Husbands now enjoy the status of a lord in a compact set-up comprising of husband, wife and a few children. The wife in that home is no more the second or the third or the youngest among the many wives within the family, but she is now the queen of her own empire.

Many of us often forget that achieving fulfilment in the conjugal life of husband and wife rests on efforts, not on chance. The institution of marriage hardly acts as an insurance for that fulfilment, let alone a guarantee. It is only a means, not an end in itself. Marriage confers a social licence and legal right to the union of man and woman, providing elbow-room and freedom from interference. One has to make it a success through tireless efforts and sacrifices. Those who regard love before marriage as the solution of all conjugal problems, are now learning the hard way that marriage by courtship is far from fool-proof, as is not the appointment of an employee after an interview.

Day after day, husband and wife influence each other through their respective tastes, habits and attitudes. They reconstruct and recreate each other every moment, after their own passion.

This giving and receiving, making and unmaking go on invisibly, unknowingly and perhaps unopposed. This becomes more easy through the closest possible togetherness; togetherness not confined in the home alone but extending over to the outside world as well.

The human mind has myriad forms, its identity is endless. Its essence is not a constant; with varying surroundings, its expressions also vary. A wife would know her husband through diverse tests he will go through—during ceremonies and festivals, in gambling, in famine, in revolution. A husband would discover his wife little by little, in ever-newer embraces, the way a gem-setter discovers the diamond, emerald or pearl in new designs on ornaments. Thus, if one's wife be the consort at co-bathing, she is perceived by her mate in such a form which is perhaps not to be found in the gracious image of the house-mistress patiently waiting every morning with a steaming cup of tea in hand. Why should they, who are not offended at the sight of their wives in the arms of other men at the dance hall, feel sorry to have her as a mate while bathing? Of course, one who grew up watching Hollywood movies would not be shocked at the sight of a female body in swim suit!

Mrs Ghose kept her word. On the way back, she halted her motorcar at the entrance to Nizamuddin. A passage to an unstudied chapter of history opened up.

Ala-ud-din, the Afghan emperor, had built a mosque at the town's end of what was then Delhi. Long after his death, one day, a fakir arrived at the mosque. The fakir was Nizamuddin Auliya. He took a fancy to the place. The great man stayed back. Gradually, his holy fame spread far and wide. Followers and devotees multiplied apace.

The scarcity of water in the nearby village drew the fakir's attention. He resolved to dig a large pond where the thirsty would quench their thirst, village belles would fill their pitchers and visitors to the mosque would do ablution before offering prayers in the mosque. But his determination was obstructed unexpectedly by the sovereign's ire. The humble fakir, Hazrat Nizamuddin Auliya, earned the wrath of the mighty Sultan Ghiyas-ud-din Tughluq.

Ghiyas-ud-din Tughluq, the founder of the Tughluq dynasty, had no touch of nobility in his ancestry. He started life as a slave. But by sheer dint of his heroism and wit, Ghiyas-ud-din Tughluq established himself as an omraha of substance even during the reign of Emperor Ala-ud-din. He became one of the Maliks of the sovereign empire.

Following the death of Ala-ud-din, two worthless sultans reigned for six years in a row, who led the country to the brink of lawlessness. At that time Ghiyas-ud-din was the Governor of Punjab. Then, Khusro Khan, a low-caste Hindu who had converted to Islam, occupied the throne of Delhi. Ghiyas-ud-din campaigned in Delhi with his army from Punjab. In the battle, he overpowered and killed Khusro Khan. Subsequently, Ghiyas-ud-din proclaimed himself the emperor.

Ghiyas-ud-din possessed stamina, strength and the dexterity required to rule. His cruelty was also frightening in the same degree. Once, some irresponsible and reckless men took to spreading the rumour of Ghiyas-ud-din's death. The baseless rumour reached the sultan. Unperturbed, he ordered his Sipah-salar, 'They've buried me falsely; I shall bury them truly'. Many unfortunates fell to their deaths in a flash; corpse-eater birds and animals had their day.

Ghiyas-ud-din had considerable prudence too. At that time, loot and massacre accompanying frequent Mughal forays and incursions were a continuous threat in northern India. With a view to defeating the objective of the attackers, Ghiyas-ud-din built a new walled township securely guarded by an impregnable fortress at the entrance. On one end was a hillock, on the other end, the walled township and in the middle, a large lake was dug. Rain water accumulated in the lake from the hill during the rainy season; the subjects of the Crown were thus assured of year-round supply of potable water.

Strife broke out between the fakir and the sultan over the building of this township; to be exact, over the construction of the wall that would surround the town.

A good many labourers were needed to dig Nizamuddin Auliya's large pond. Thousands of labourers were needed to build Ghiyas-ud-din Tughluq's new township. But the number of available labourers in Delhi was far too few to meet both needs at the same time. It was perfectly natural that the sultan desired that his work should be finished first and until then, the digging of the pond by donating labour would lie in waiting. An emperor's might lay in wealth, which was measurable. A fakir's strength is sourced from his selfless heart, which is immeasurable. Numerous labourers, of their own, gave their enterprise gratis and digging of the *talao* of Nizamuddin proceeded apace. The sultan was enraged at this.

But, before he could act on it, the call was sounded for another immediate task at hand. He had to rush to Bengal with troops and arms to quell a rebellion there.

Prince Muhammad Tughluq remained in the capital as the caretaker sovereign. He was an admirer of Nizamuddin. By dint of the prince's favour, the digging of the pond of the selfless saint continued day and night and it was filled with water before long. Tughlaqabad's wall remained unfinished.

At last, the time for return of the sultan came near. Nizamuddin's disciples advised him to flee from there. The fakir smiled, '*Dilli dur ast*' (Delhi is a far cry!). The sultan was covering a *yojan* daily; his distance from the capital was shortening fast. Nizamuddin's disciples, extremely concerned, were advising him, daily, to escape. Daily, the fakir smiled and assured them, '*Dilli dur ast*' (Delhi is a far cry!)

Then, a day came when it was only a day's journey before the sultan would enter the capital. All disciples of Nizamuddin pleaded with him fervently for the last time to flee and save his precious life. Ghiyas-ud-din's rage and cruelty were known to all. They imagined the meeting and were scared to the bone at the thought of the violent fate of the saint at the hands of the sultan. With a smile on his lips, the fearless, all-possessions-forsaken saint replied calmly on that last day, '*Dilli dur ast*' (Delhi is a far cry!) With complete detachment, he continued to count the beads of the rosary in hand.

Muhammad had erected a richly decorated stage to welcome his father at the entrance to the capital city. The canopy was made of rich velvet. It was rendered glittering by an intricate inlay work of precious stones with thread works of silver and gold. Muhammad strived to make it a grand event of utmost pomp and grandeur—varieties of music hands, busy armies of men, amirs and omrahas, all together made it a very colourful assembly. A lavish and sumptuous dinner was to be served followed by an exhibition parade of elephant troops would follow dinner.

At the centre of the stage, at a little elevated rostrum, was the seat of the emperor, flanked by a couple of seats for his successors. At cow-dust hour the next day, the Sultan entered the stage erected to welcome him. He took his seat amidst huge applaud. He took by his side his favourite younger son to sit. Not Muhammad, but his younger brother.

Dining over, Muhammad very politely sought the permission of the emperor to start the exhibition parade. He was the master of the parade which would start with emperor's kind consent. Ghiyas-ud-din smilingly nodded his approval.

Muhammad calmly exited the stage with measured steps.

Bang! Crash! Thud!

A swing of an elephant's head displaced a pillar. In no time, the entire stage collapsed to the ground with a huge thud.

Numerous wooden pillars flew all over the place. The wails of men who fell under the fallen pillars rent the dark night-sky. Clouds of dust that arose shrouded the vision. Uncounted many were crushed under the feet of startled elephants that ran amok. Amidst that baffling chaos, rescue workers looked in vain for the emperor.

On the following morning, the corpse of the emperor was discovered under the rubble of the broken-down stage. His two hands covered the lifeless body of the beloved son whom he had chosen successor to the throne in his mind. Perhaps he wanted to save the life of his dearest using his own body as a shield.

Thus the end fell on Ghiyas-ud-din just outside the town, in his son's company, when he was at the acme of worldly possessions and fame and wielded a mighty influence across a huge empire. Delhi remained forever beyond the reach of his footfall.

'Dilli dur ast' (Delhi is a far cry!).

Four

Even to this day, a visitor's first glimpse, on entering the dargah of Nizamuddin, is of the lake dug by him. Walking by the lake, we reached a spacious area at the centre of which lay the grave of the fakir. Over and around the tomb were built beautiful edifices and alleyways. At a later epoch in history, Emperor Shah Jahan had built around the tomb, marble arches and columns and had surrounded the courtyard with cobwebbed and intricately designed stone walls. Akbar II had erected the dome over the tomb. Emperors felt obliged in associating their name with the name of the holy fakir.

Tughlaqabad, Ghiyas-ud-din's capital, is today a stupendous ruin. The BBCI railway line runs past it. This place now holds an appeal only to archaeologists and tourists. At the dargah of Nizamuddin, a fair happens each year, even today. Devotees throng there from far-flung corners. The former royal capital with its towering pride has long been levelled to dust; the glory of the poor monk has remained undiminished through the reverential remembrance of the devotees over generations. Its attraction stretches into the far future.

Akin to the final desire held by the devout Hindus of breathing one's last by the holy Ganges, the wealthy residents of Delhi have yearned over centuries to be buried in the vicinity of Auliya's tomb, desiring the proximity of 'Mir Majlis' in afterlife. So, the place is replete with countless tombs of amirs and omrahas. One such tomb contains the remains of the poet Amir Khusro.

Khusro's genius was unmatched; his fame, widespread. In the poetry-circles of Delhi, he was incomparable. He had a deeply cordial relation with Khijir Khan, the poetry-loving son of Ala-ud-din. He composed, in his own peerless meter, the heroic exploits of Khijir Khan, bestowing on it timeless appeal.

In an adjacent cemetery in Nizamuddin lay the remains of another poet whose works have no rival in Urdu literature. The tomb of poet Ghalib is simple. It is covered only with a slab of ordinary stone. The corpus of nineteenth century Urdu literature bears an unfading memory of him in his poems and lore. Plenty of rich edifices are built in the world to adorn the tombs of men of little consequence. But the onus of erecting the memorial is always on the poet himself.

Building a memorial was not a practice in the era of the Hindus. It was so because the Hindus had more interest in afterlife rather than in this mortal life. So it never occurred to them to erect a mausoleum at the cremation ground for perpetuating the memories of near and dear ones. Not a single Hindu royal built a memorial from the time of the Mughals to the time of Prithviraj. None of the Rajput royals erected any likeness of Itmad-ud-daula, Safdarjung, or Humayun's tomb. They dug water tanks, built temples, offered cows and land to the Brahmins. It was meant for the good of the world. Emperor Ashok built the Ashokan Pillar for public instruction, not to spread his name. Buddha built chaityas and viharas for utility of the Sangha, Sankarcharya built missions with a mind to spread the study of *Vedanta*.

Devotion was the last word in Hindu life at that time. Like a blooming sunflower; all action, thought, pursuit and attention were directly or indirectly aimed towards the name of the god. As the central idea of life was then to regard the wife and son as only illusory relations, what would one do with romance? They believed that the entire manifest world is pervaded by maya or illusion. Consequently, one's father has become 'the ultimate venerable'; the spouse, 'husband divine'; the wife a 'co-religious follower'. It's difficult to guess whether romantic love or desire for divine bliss in the afterlife motivated women to sacrifice themselves in their late husband's pyre. Royal princesses, privileged to elect their husbands, scarcely settled on their choice by falling in love. Princess Sanjukta garlanded Prince Prithviraj for his fame and wealth, like a young maiden of this era who puts the engagement ring on an ICS officer's finger.

Islam introduced a different ideal in life. Deliverance through sacrifice was not theirs. They cared little for afterlife and made this mortal life the be-all and end-all of existence. They lived to enjoy, shed tears, made others weep and to top it all, they loved. So they looted for the sake of women, they robbed to serve the cause of love; they killed and resorted to many misdeeds to please their beloved. No doubt, many of these acts do not deserve support. But, does love ever care for anyone's sanction? Or follow dictums of morality? Did Ahalya await society's sanction or the support of scriptures? Did Arjuna of the *Mahabharata*? Did Kanu of Vrindavan? Was it the priority for Rizia Begum, Mary Waleuska or Lady Hamilton?

The Muslims wanted to keep the memories of their beloveds alive for ever. They wanted to build memorials. So they have erected mausoleums on the tombs of their fathers, husbands, wives and even for their paramours. The Hindus were worshippers, they have given us the Vedas and the Upanishads. The Muslims are artisans, they have given us the Taj and the Rangmahal. The Hindus are meditative, they have given us philosophy. The Muslims are practitioners, they have given us music. The Hindus pride over their heads and the Muslims pride over their hearts. The duo have woven the past of India, so would it be for her future too.

Taking away anyone of the two would lead to Pakistan, even if Mr Mohammed Ali Jinnah disapproves of it.

My co-traveller drew my attention to a small marble tomb. It was of Jahanara, the daughter of the Emperor.

History has it that the rule of Alamgir bears irrevocable black spots in its records of persecution of people practising other beliefs and religions; it is recorded in all school texts. However, the world does not know much about the heavy curses cast on this heartless yet immensely powerful warrior king, by the despairing sighs of his two remarkable lady captives.

Both Jahanara and Zebunnisa were Aurangzeb's close relatives. One was his younger sister and the other, his daughter. Both were beautiful, unusually courageous and forthright in manner. Both were unwed and had spent much of their time in Aurangzeb's prisons.

But these two ill-fated women had another deep similarity. Both were poets; they were the noted poetesses of the Mughal era.

Jahanara's works were not preserved with care. Like flowers which fall to ground, after blooming in secrecy in deep forests, beyond the reach of human appreciation and knowledge, her works were reduced to dust. Only a few samples of her talent are strewn hither and thither.

The poetic fame of Zebunnisa is more widespread. A real talent in poetics is evident in her work '*Zeb-ul Monsha'at*'. Many writers have ascribed the authorship of the famous Persian book of verse '*Diwan-e Makhfi*' to Zebunnisa; pundits, however, are sceptic of this claim today.

Jahanara has captured my fancy since childhood. I would have to spend long nights before the history exam, trying my best, to mug up the Mughal period, thorny with references of numerous dates. Sleepiness overtook me often, the body became idle, the head swayed in drowsiness. In that condition, I tried to imagine Jahanara's features whenever I read the episode on her.

In her first flush of youth, she enjoyed the pre-eminence of a princess in full measure. She indisputably ruled the harem. She distributed favours and rulings undeterred. She was the dearest among the daughters of Emperor Shah Jahan. The emperor built the Jama Masjid of Delhi, the largest prayer house of the Muslims in India, for her.

Jahanara had a favorite female slave. One day, her clothing caught fire inadvertently. In her attempt to quell the fire, the princess burnt herself seriously. Medicine men of all hues gathered in Delhi to cure her without effect. The princess's life was threatened.

Anxious Shajahan sent for a sahib doctor. The physcian was Gabriel Boughton, the medicine man of the *kuthi* at Surat. Boughton said that he must examine the patient before prescribing any medicine. This surprised the courtiers. What nonsense! Didn't the idiot know how to pay obeisance to the zenana of the venerable emperor?

But at long last, paternal love won over social norm. Shah Jahan agreed to the proposal of Boughton. Jahanara recovered to health in a short time. On her request, Shah Jahan,wanted to award Boughton anything he might want.

Bowing to the ground before the emperor, Boughton said that he had nothing to ask for himself. He prayed for a piece of land at Balasore, hundred and four miles south of Calcutta, to build a *kuthi* for the English traders there and with that, the right to transact business duty free in this country.

Boughton's prayer was granted. This great example of goodwill for one's own country has only one more match in modern times. That is of the Jewish scientist, Dr Kyme Weissman.

In 1916, during the critical period of the First World War, England ran short of acetone, the unexceptionable chemical ingredient for production of explosives; a professor of Manchester University took upon himself the responsibility of producing acetone artificially. Prime Minister Lloyd George insisted, 'Professor, the fate of England rests on your success or failure. I want quick action and quick result.'

The professor assured him, 'As you say, Sir.'

Working day and night he invented the method of producing acetone artificially in a few weeks and saved Britain from conceding defeat in the war.

Overwhelmed, the Prime Minister wanted to award him the highest prize.

Weissman rejected his offer with humility.

Lloyd George asked him again, 'Peerage? Money?'

'No, Sir. I've only one thing to ask for. I seek from you a country for the people of my faith, a nation for the Jews.'

Sometime after, in the Balfour Declaration, a home for the Jews was carved out in Palestine. Of course, it was on paper. The Jews are not properly settled there even today. Rather, nowadays the Conservatives are pursuing the policy of maintaining the hegemony of Arabs in Palestine to preserve their influence in the Middle-East. The word thankfulness is found in the language of the English, not really in their character.

The English laid the foundations of trade in India, without a contest, through the magnanimity of Jahanara, the foundation of the empire was strengthened hidden from all eyes. The same English have written a history blemishing the character of Jahanara. This is not that surprising. The civilian who has built a house in Staffordshire with the pension benefit accrued from his Indian service, is often the most vociferous critic of India. Leopold Emery is the greatest enemy of India's freedom struggle—because he was born in Gorakhpur.

The last scenes of the drama of Jahanara's life are tragic.

Among all his sons, Darashikoh was the most beloved of his father Shah Jahan. But Darashikoh showed predilection for Christianity. This was far from fetching admiration in Islamic circles. Receiving the tidings of his father's illness, Suja set out for Delhi, militarily equipped. Dara defeated him in the battle of Varanasi. Aurangzeb then confabulated with Morad. He gave Morad to understand that he was beyond the vice-grip of this sinful, greedy and illusory world they lived in. He supposed, if they teamed up to defeat Dara in battle, then, if Shah Jahan was dead —may the Almighty prevent that from happening—the throne of Delhi would go to Morad. The drunkard Morad placed his faith in Aurangzeb's assurances. Dara was defeated and fled to Punjab, on a festive night's end, the intoxicated Morad was taken prisoner. Aurangzeb declared himself the Emperor. He imprisoned his father Shah Jahan and kept him confined in a little cell at Agra fort.

Aurangzeb wanted to bestow the dignity of a Begum of the Badshah to Jahanara. But she chose co-imprisonment with her father, Shah Jahan, with a view to nursing his needs. In that hour in history, when ruthless fraudulence and unbridled treachery had gathered all around like dense darkness, only Jahanara would remain illumined as a steady, unwavering little flame. Shah Jahan's second daughter, Roshanara, took sides with Aurangzeb and became his favourite. Her garden is situated in the Civil Lines of Delhi. Recently, Roshanara Club has come up there, to serve as the Monte Carlo of Delhi. The club has earned notoreity in northern India as the venue to play bridge at a stake of ten rupees.

Days pass, months follow. Six seasons rotate in a cycle. Summer goes by with its heat and fiery storms. The long shadows of dark cloudy days of the rainy-season descend over the Yamuna. Pet peacocks dance in joy in the alleyways of the palace. In the light and shadow of autumn morning, the *kas* flowers on the river bank wave in the breeze. A dewy season wraps the landscape in mist; winter brings heartbreak. Flowers sway on the branches and twigs of *siris* trees with the advent of spring. Behind the high wall of the palace at Agra, another year is added in the captive life of Jahanara, one more year sheds from the span of her life. In lone, work-free hours, the princess composes poetry, all lost in herself.

One night, a beautiful parcel reached Shah Jahan from Aurangzeb. The son had sent a gift to his father. Could it be the first sign of repentance? Old Shah Jahan opened it with quivering hands. After removing layer after layer of wrappers, finally rolled over to ground the severed head of his beloved son Darashikoh. The emperor fell unconscious on Jahanara's lap.

Jahanara nursed Shah Jahan till his end. She nursed her immobile father with singular devotion and patience. After his death, she returned to Delhi.

Finally, on one holy Ramadan day, the royal prisoner gained her freedom in the realm of calm, cold death. She was buried, in fulfilment of her wish, by the side of the tomb of Nizamuddin Auliya. There is neither a structure, nor a cover, not a trace of worldly wealth anywhere near her grave. Only a poem, composed by her, is inscribed on it,

> 'Please ensure only grass adorns my grave; for a
> poor wretch like me that would be the ideal cover.'

This, indeed, is the fittest entombment of the impermanent identity of Shah Jahan's daughter Jahanara who had been a follower of saint Nizamuddin Auliya in life and death.

In the tranquil silence of the approaching evening, we three visitors stood in reverence before the tomb. None spoke, but our hearts were laden.

Young green grass covers the unembellished small grave. Little drops of dew from the clear blue sky accumulate over it in the night, the first crimson rays of the rising sun touch it in the early morning and the golden-hued glow of the cow-dust hour spreads over the tomb in the evening. Do they receive the soft fragrance of the tender body buried under centuries ago? Do they feel the soft murmur of the devotee heart which once pulsated beneath her youthful bosom any longer?

Five

The biggest sensation of the morning. A local newspaper has published in its morning edition, the summary of Cripps' proposals. It quotes extensively from its own correspondent's reliable source. It is learnt that the government is upset at the publication of this news and top bosses of the Investigation Department are on the keen pursuit of this 'reliable source'.

A furore occurred among journalists. All of us have been getting the hints of the contents of the mission for the last few days. We didn't disclose anything, with due respect to what was a gentleman's agreement. The British and the American journalists covering the event inferred that this might have been leaked by a Hon'ble member of the Viceroy's Council.

The popular belief is that on the day of arrival of Cripps, the Hon'ble Members of the Viceroy's Council were waiting in the Viceroy's house, starving since half past twelve, to greet him. Cripps arrived at 2:00 pm. Lord Linlithgow introduced his colleagues, standing in a row next to him, to Cripps. All that Cripps did was shake their hands, disinterestedly reciting, 'How do you do?' Then, without a second word, he departed for his assigned suite.

They expected that Cripps would discuss his proposals with them, take their opinions, before sitting with the leaders. This hope was also belied. The Cripps Mission remained unrevealed. So it is not surprising that they were rather annoyed. Be they executive councillors, after all, they were human beings! According to hearsay, at last, through the good offices of the Viceroy, Cripps briefed the summary of his Mission to them at a dinner party last night at the Viceroy's palace. An enterprising 'own correspondent' of a newspaper made the briefings public in 'his' own words this morning. If the presence of fire is inferred from smoke in the mountain, the suspicion of the foreign correspondents as to the source of the leak has some weight.

Journalists do have the right to a 'scoop'. Even in exercising this right, an unwritten borderline is maintained. Where, there is at stake, the wider interest of a nation or a people, a journalist's own sense of discretion is at work in censoring his copy. I clearly remember the event of the abdication of the throne by Edward the VIII. The press of Britain was aware of the affairs of Mrs Simpson and Edward since May that year. This was heard by many on the grapevine of Fleet Street. No newspaper, however, printed it. There was no government-imposed restriction, nor any legal ruling against printing it. As of now, a Second Front is expected to be formed against Germany, any time, in the war. Stuart Gelder or Drew Pearson may gain access to the information where the allied power will strike next. They will never break that news, although it would not be a lesser 'scoop' than the Cripps proposals.

Of all questions, the central one is of honesty. Cripps made a sincere plea in the name of Britain and India's welfare. We all agreed to it without protest. Now, an Indian journalist broke that promise by scooping the story. So, we Indians are ashamed. If gentlemen might be journalists, why might journalists not be gentlemen?

Cripps has shifted residence from the Viceroy's house to a bungalow at no. 3, Queen Victoria Road. This is assigned to Sir Andrew Chloe, Member of the Viceroy's Council. Chloe is the next governor designate for Assam. He has gone on two months' leave to Mussouri or, maybe, to Almorah, for a rest, before taking over the plum charge of governor.

The residences of the executive councillors are government-owned. Pretty, single-storied, veranda-houses; painted light yellow, with a large lawn in front. It's so big that an East Bengal–Mohun Bagan match might be played inside there after putting goalposts at the two ends. Neatly mowed, soft green grass covers the ground. There is a round flower bed in the middle. A bright-red cobbled road encircles it; motorcars can take turns there easily. On one side of the entrance to the bungalow, a house-number is painted on the glass in large numerals. A small hole beside it houses a lantern to enable passers-by to read the number, with its light, from a distance in the night. Cars are parked in the porch adjacent to the veranda. On either side of the veranda are two small rooms which house the offices of the secretary and the stenographer of the Hon'ble Member.

The six bungalows are exactly alike. Standing by the two roads, King Edward Road and Queen Victoria Road, which stretch out like two hands in front of the Secretariat, these houses are, as though, six identical twins, sextuplet companions to the Dionne quintuplets[2].

The planning of the city of New Delhi has, in it, the example of reducing something really good to an object of ridicule by excesses. The monomaniac fixity of the architects of the city on uniformity in design has lent it an appearance of mould-casting in place of beauty; have made barracks for houses indeed. 'Creation' demands expression of underlying unity through diversity in forms. Any attempt to bring harmony by equating dimensions alone is mere copying. We call him 'Brahma' who does the former and 'Viswakarma', who pursues the latter. The first has 'art' in it and the other, 'craft'.

In ancient times, the king was at the heart of town-planning. Depending on the king's location and preferences, the town flourished. With the royal palace at the centre, ministers and other important royals built their palatial mansions, commoners built their dwellings and traders adorned their shops and establishments. With the rise and fall of the royal dynasties, capitals also shared its fate; it either flourished or decayed.

Unmistakable evidence of these occurences are seen even today—in Agra, Aurangabad and Fatehpur Sikri.

In today's world, commerce is more valued than empire building. The glory of the king—like that of the husband of the lady physician—now lies, not in his own valour, but on the extent of commerce and trade of his subjects. Not only in India, in other countries as well, the weighing scales of the traders evolve into the sceptre of the ruler overnight—either in the trader's own identity, or using several other assumed names. So, the 'centre of gravity' in modern-day 'mega' cities, lies in Clive Street or Hornby Road. Their source of inspiration is the chamber of commerce rather than the chamber of princes. So New York is more important than Washington, Kanpore overshadows Lucknow, Tatanagar overtakes Patna.

In modern India, New Delhi happens to be the only city which is not lorded over by a stock exchange. Neither are there the Vaishyas, nor the Brahmins. There are only Kshatriyas, the warrior classes. Of course, their arsenal has changed. Modern Kshatriyas live on words, not swords. Ancient Kshatriyas ripened their skills by arraying fortifications. The length, breadth and radius were governed by rules. The modern Kshatriyas end up with their hair and beards ripened through dealing in files, which are also guided by similar precedent norms. Consequently, the roads, the buildings, the houses and all other elements of New Delhi's layout, seem to be making an effort to be identical. Be it shops, markets, roads, parks, residential quarters, or roadside rows of blackberry trees, all stand stiff and upright like khaki-clad platoons of soldiers, positioned at attention, with raised bayonets.

Cripps' meetings were held in his new residence with his aides and advisors in tow. Professor Coupland of Oxford and the Canadian socialist Graham Spry were among them.

I was introduced to Coupland in a debate meeting in London. He is keen on the affairs of India; whether he is liberal enough, I don't know.

Cripps received Maulana Azad, Gandhiji, Pandit Nehru and Mr Jinnah, one by one. Another Muslim Congressman accompanied Maulana Azad as an interpreter. He was Mr Asaf Ali. Asaf Ali's place of birth was the United Provinces, his place of work is Delhi and the home of his in-laws is Bengal. His wife, Aruna Asaf Ali, had the Bengali surname 'Ganguly' before marriage. She is a close relation of Meera Devi, the youngest daughter of Tagore.

Pandit Jawaharlal Nehru's knowledge of English is as well known as his patriotism. Many a critic of English origin has admitted that his skill and style of writing English is rare even among living English writers. Although the English used by Gandhiji is not of as great a literary value as that of Jawaharlal, the clarity of expression and the lucid beauty of plainspeak embodied in his use of the language often reminds one of the Bible. Mr Jinnah was an established barrister. His dexterity of questioning in English is outstanding. There was only one man who spoke in his own mother tongue while conversing with Cripps. It was in Urdu, not in English; albeit, the speaker's fairly good working knowledge of English is an oft-spoken fact. Maulana has his own original style, indeed. Glory be to him!

English is not our mother tongue; we are required to learn it. This is not bothersome. Possibly, it often proves profitable. We have gained an exposure to and received most of the modern concept of nationalism through our learning of English. But in our society, the ability to speak and write in English has become the yardstick of one's education, intelligence and achievements. This is silly. He, who writes the answer paper well in English in college, gains adoration everywhere, in the job market as well as with the mother of a nubile marriageable daughter. So, we are all overjoyed and gratified when a foreign visitor commends that an Indian leader speaks 'faultless English'. Maulana Azad's gesture protests most eloquently against this mentality. Irrespective of the speaker being Cripps, the Viceroy, or George the V himself, whoever would like to converse with me but not use my language, wilfully or otherwise, why should it be that I must feel obliged to use his language? Bravo to Azad!

Gandhiji exited from Cripps' chamber almost after three hours. Cripps accompanied him up the stairs of the veranda. In a moment, all journalists circled him in a trap. Full of curiosity, they were agog with excitement and anxiety. He welcomed them with a smile and silenced many questions without a word.

Cripps has a good sense of humour. He added to the suspense with his comment that the journalists should not infer on the positive or negative of Cripps' Proposals from Gandhiji's smile alone, because he'd tutored Gandhiji to flash a smile while leaving. A big roll of laughter followed.

But there does exist stickier people on earth, even more so than insurance agents, the priests of Kashi or matchmakers. They are reporters. They fired questions about Gandhiji's discussions. Pointing to Cripps, the Mahatma answered, 'Please ask him. I've nothing to say.'

A seasoned reporter quipped, 'Are the proposals so outrageous that you are rendered speechless?'

'You naughty boy', he replied and with a pleasant smile, put an end to the discussions. Alighting his vehicle, he greeted everybody with clasped hands and left for Birla House.

The Information Department has opened a camp office in a small side room for the benefit of reporters. We, the reporters, invade the place with abundant energy each morning, mid-day, afternoon and evening, although the information available is limited to the time and date of meetings that various Indian leaders have scheduled with Cripps and nothing more.

The camp office is headed by Jagdish Natarajan, the son of K. S. Natarajan, the famous journalist from Bombay and the founder of the 'Indian Social Reformer'. He has joined the government after leaving the *Pioneer*'s board of editors. He knows many facts about the political history of India. He speaks English fluently and is unaffected by the usual distortions of the Tamilian tongue. I was invited to a dinner at his home one night.

Natarajan's homemaker is not from Madras; she is an Anglo-Indian. Her paternal family—the Bobbs—are famous for playing tennis and her maternal ancestry is rooted in Bengal. Her grandmother had the Bengali surname Banerjee before marriage, which gives her a claim to a certain nobility if one were to go by the caste hierarchy established by Ballal Sen. Playing the piano is her forte.

In many such progressive Bengali families, moorings within Indian culture are not very apparent. The breadwinner of the family, in most of these cases, might have been educated abroad. After completing English studies at Oxford, medicine in Edinburgh or law at Lincoln's Inn, he returns to India and establishes himself in his own profession, earning profusely. He likes his suit, loves his soup and lounges on a couch. His homemaker throws parties, attends the club and plays bridge with male friends unhesitatingly. In their homes, the servant is 'boy,' the mother of the children is 'Memsaheb' and the young daughter is 'Missybaba'.

Those who act sahib without even going to England are even fiercer. Like those Muslims who joined the League from the Congress. Sleeping without wearing sleeping-suits or eating without fork and spoon is as barbaric to them as consigning infants into the Ganges or the system of Sati!

Yet, one can't deny that nothing compares to the manner in which we are extracted from the root of our culture, by marrying an English or Anglo-Indian bride. However short a Bengali wife might trim her hair, gulp gimlets or speak wrong English in an affected Anglo style, pursing her coloured lips holding a burning cigarette, her basic culture lies hidden beneath her skin although it might be rubbed over with Coty or Max Factor. Her blood carries the red corpuscles of blind faith transmuted from her foremothers. So, a date for a daughter's marriage is consulted from the traditional almanac, the recovery of an ailing husband is pawned to a goddess in lieu of token sacrifices, the welfare of children is linked to fasting on the sixth lunar day. Notwithstanding consuming steak and veal in hotels, men conduct the last rites of their parents faithfully, following tradition, under the family priest's direction.

Most unfortunate are the children of Indian fathers and European mothers. They are estranged from their father's circle and eschewed by their mother's society. They belong neither to India nor to England. To which country will they bear patriotism, for which nation will they feel empathy? They receive their surname from their father, the complexion from their mother; from whom will they receive their mindset? They are truly cultural cross-products, not only by birth but also in physique and nature. None of the children born of wedlock between an Indian and an European, to this day, has proven original merit in the arts, literature, science or music. At most, their achievements are limited to holding the post of a general manager in the Railways or a director in the Telegraph Department.

European society is substantially based on common participation. This takes the same form from England to Italy. The same type of dress, the same kind of milieu, the same set of manners and code of conduct are shared by, for example, the English, French, Czech and Hungarians. All over Europe, people sit for their breakfast, lunch, dinner and supper strictly by the clock and use knives and forks while eating. They go to the movies or plays on Saturday nights, pray devoutly on their knees in churches on Sundays. But for linguistic diversity, an affinity in social customs rule all over Europe. I've seen that in London, an Austrian wife of an English husband is as easily accepted in society as an English one and there is hardly any difference in the way of leading a family life with their husbands, sons and daughters. Their children grow up exactly like the other Dicks, Pauls and Harringtons of English society.

Well, it's not entirely trouble free. The troubles, not visible in daily life, hound the minds of husband and wife on special occasions. For example, which team would be supported during an Ashes match in the Lord's by an English husband and an Australian wife? Whose win in the war would bring cheer to a German Mr and whose loss would bring grief to his Russian Mrs?

If, in the future, a United States of Europe takes shape and the language of common speech becomes one, it is not difficult to imagine there would be a greater number of conjugal unions among the different European States. Spanish youths would often then marry Norwegian brides, the way it is, at present, between the Scotch and the Welsh. It would be an everyday affair, like a bride from Konnagar in Bengal taken home by a groom hailing from Barishal.

The values and objectives of existence in India and Europe are different, so are its structures in the social order. Not to speak of the joint-family system, our society is not limited to an individual and his wife and children. Its influence and networks are far-flung among many relatives, in-laws and kinsmen, linked through a variety of duty boundness and responsibilities. Spate in conjugal unions between the Orient and the Occident, although capable of bringing happiness in individual cases, is unlikely to bring about a social union between the two continents. All European females are to be regarded by us, for our own welfare, as other men's wives.

I've been introduced to a Maharashtrian Brahmin gentleman at the dinner given by Mr Natarajan. He is well over forty; grey patches outnumber black ones on his head; he has a strong physique, wide forehead and a sharp nose. Most wonderful are his eyes. His large, deep eyes resemble that of Arjun in the Indian painting by Abani Tagore; it bears the mark of untold weariness. His gaze has, in it, the radiance of intelligence no doubt, but what overshadows it is a dark, solemn shade, similar to the rain-bearing dense clouds in the rainy season. This kind of exceptional eyes are not commonly seen in men.

But in the society of New Delhi, the fame of Charudutt Adharkar is associated with drinks. In one go, he may drink, at ease, ten pegs of whiskey. His eyelids won't even quiver. It is not an invincible feat, indeed. There are one or two others who can do that too. But it was not only in taking drinks, Adharkar excels in devising cocktails also. Charudutt knows countless mixing ratios. Numerous methods of preparing cocktails are at his fingertips. Hostesses of parties and dinners consult a-priori with Adharkar. He also shares his knowledge with great pleasure. 'Who are coming? How many? If you want to kill in three rounds, then first serve rum-orange, then gin and lime. Finally, serve whiskey. For the ladies, you might serve brandy with ginger ale in between. What, you don't know how to mix rum-orange? What a pity! Well, note it down. Take one-quarter Italian vermouth in the shaker. Oh, no Italian? Well, take French then. Add one-quarter orange juice to it and then add one-half rum. Mix in sufficient ice and a dash of cinnamon extract. Done! Stir it well and serve in cocktail glasses.'

Mrs Natarajan tipped me, 'Minisahib, (my *nom de choix* Minisahib has spread out from Sensaheb's home to the outside world through the good-humoured references of my well-wishers) in case you would like to taste newer cocktails, take a suggestion or two from Mr Adharkar.'

Adharkar replied smiling, 'Yes, I've an idea that after my retirement from service, I'll obtain patents for my recipes. Then I'll insert an ad in the newspaper—"If it's a drink, consult Adharkar."

Like the ubiquitous Mrs Beaton's book of recipes and kitchen art, a copy of Adharkar's *Book of Drinks* will adorn the bookshelves of the homes of newlyweds.'

But, for me, a bigger surprise than all this was waiting to be revealed. After dinner was over, pressed by sincere requests of the guests, Adharkar played a tune on the violin. It was based on the Indian classical raga *Darbari Kanada*. He played only the overture. He was at it for almost twenty minutes, playing a perfect rendition. When he finished, he asked, looking at me, 'Can you identify the tune, Minisahib?'

I was so taken aback that I forgot to answer. He spoke in clear Bengali.

'What? Are you shocked?' This, too, he asked in Bengali.

I avoided his query and said, 'You're strange. How did you learn Bengali so well?'

'Is this a worthy question? How did you learn English?'

'Well, I learnt it to earn a living.'

'I learnt it to save my soul. No, no, no more questions; curiosity is a feminine vice.'

He shook hands sincerely before departure and said, 'Minisahib, hope you are not angry with me for having addressed you informally! You must be much younger in age. I live at Rotendum Road, no. 22. Come one evening, I'll speak Bengali, I'll play violin and I'll serve you Top-Hat. Do you know Top-Hat? Oh! You don't? One-half gin, one-quarter French vermouth, one-quarter Italian. A drop of bitters, stirred with a good deal of ice.'

I did visit Adharkar at his address. Not enticed by Top-Hat but drawn by the man's amazing attractions. One day, then another and then daily. In a short time we grew so intimate that had he not been a man, a scandal could well have tarnished my name through rumour mongers. If he had a nubile daughter, the housewives of New Delhi could spend idle afternoon hours gossiping over my suitability as a suitor for his daughter.

Not to speak of a daughter, there was no trace of even a daughter's mother in the household of the unwed Adharkar. His home government consisted of a few servants, a bearer and cook. Only the charge of the Revenue Department was his own; the rest—the executive, the legislative and even the judiciary—were the charges of his servants. Truly a republican arrangement! It might also be termed 'republifun' for the servants.

We argue, we discuss politics, religion, war strategy, no subject is kept out of purview. Off and on, poetry becomes the subject of discussion. Numerous poetry and quotations by Tagore are committed to the memory of Adharkar. He recites in a deep tone, 'I've swapped heart with many, suffered a thousand deaths and chimed like anklets on many a feet.' Then, he asks, looking at me, 'Tell me, where can one find it?' If I can answer, he says, 'Well done! Now you've earned a drink. Hey boy, get sahib...' On some other occasion, he might say, 'Today it's your test. Tell me, where would you find – "Time and again, in this life, I've roamed, beseeching her who might call me back; that woman in varying forms, with a smile, opened her door continually"'.

'Failed? Well, I give you five more minutes. What, you still can't? Ha Ha! Being a Bengali, you lose in bets on Bengali poetry to a non-Bengali! What would people say? Better have your head cleared! Boy, get one Brooklyn! Fill half a tumbler with pieces of ice, mix in one-quarter French vermouth and one-quarter dry gin. Stir it hard and then add two drops of orange bitters. It's delicious.'

One day he asked, 'Minisahib, have you ever fallen in love?'

'No.'

'What? Young man! You stayed in the UK and never fell in love! Who is going to believe this?'

'One should believe it. There are more things in heaven and earth!'

'But, there are more girls in Piccadilly and Leicester Square , that's a fact, isn't it?'

'I'll tell you the fact of the matter. Falling in love makes one look very foolish, I've seen it in the movies. In fear of this image I didn't dare to proceed.'

Adharkar burst out in laughter. 'Looks foolish, ha, ha, ha! Just imagine the reason for not falling in love! Even Bernard Shaw could not have put it better. You are a genius. No, I must get you something new today, to save my honour. Try Rum-Bruit. Four spoonfuls rum, one spoon lime, a dash of sugar, mixed with half a cup of black coffee. It's wonderful.'

My amazement grows by the day. Attachment to this Maharashtrian Brahmin develops by degrees. His life is strange. He is an ace violinist and a connoisseur of poetics, literature, music and arts. He earns a lot, spends a lot more. Most of it is spent on spirits, for own consumption and for offering and cheering others. Yet, I have not ever found him acting indecently. He takes pride in saying, 'Minisahib, your famous novelist Sarat Chatterjee wrote, "He who drinks, he must have been drunk at least on one occasion. He who denies it, he either tells lies or drinks water instead!" Sarat Chatterjee has not met Charudutt Adharkar. Had he met me, he would have taken out those lines from his novel.'

The fact that Adharkar has no wife is known to one and all. But, what about his relatives? Nobody has any idea. Through his flair for fun, frolic, hilarity, chatting and story-mongering, he enlivens all associations and parties, jazzes up the daily assembly of friends at home. Yet, looking into his eyes one seems to know, all these antics are only a façade. As though the burden of an unknown profound tragedy remains hidden somewhere in those sentient eyes, lowered by feelings; nay, episodes of untold sorrows hide behind his lone life. But Adharkar avoids questions artfully and recites instead,

'For fear of being taken in easily, I play on feelings;
He, who radiates laughter, inside him is tears.'

Six

When two Britons come together, they establish a club; when two Scotsmen meet, they open a bank; two Japanese launch a secret society. What happens when two Bengalis come together? Is it fracas? No doubt; maybe, a bit too much of it. In addition, they do one more thing. They set up a Kali temple. There is hardly any town in Northern India with a Bengali populace, which goes without a Kali temple.

Among the Hindu deities, the goddess Kali does not have a pleasing form. The beauty of the Veena-playing goddess Saraswati or the charm of goddess Laxmi seated on a lotus are not seen in the ink-black form of goddess Kali. Goddess Durga has ten arms and an equal number of weapons. But her appearance is much more soothing and graceful in comparison to the iconic representation of Kali. She wears round her neck a garland of human heads, her waist is girded with a wreath of severed human hands, in one hand she holds an open blade, in the other swings a cut-off head. Her large, wide face does not have any touch of softness, neither do her eyes suggest a tender look. Her breasts are exposed, unadorned is her body. Her tongue lolls out. Native devotees say, the Mother is dreadful; Katherine Mayo writes in her book, she is terrible.

Bengalis love this austere, frightful image. The flow of devotion introduced by Sri Chaitanya left its mark only through one particular sect. Devotees of Kali have spread out all over the land. Her worshippers are not confined only to the religious sect of the Shaktas. Obeisance to her is paid everywhere—from the hut of illiterate and rustic farmers to the palace of the rich. The Kapaliks, sitting on corpses in ancient times, worshipped Devi Kalika; the Tantriks venerated Mother Shyama; dacoits have carried out many robberies after praying to the image of the goddess adorned with a garland of beheaded human heads and seeking her blessings. In contemporary times too, Bengali women often promise sacrifices and offerings to goddess Kali in lieu of the recovery of relatives from illnesses; when epidemics break out, citizens worship the goddess with earnest simple devotion for relief. Shri Ramakrishna meditated on her in Dakshineswar; Ramprasad composed profound songs in deference to her.

This sort of a fancy for goddess Kali in the hearts of the Bengalis may appear surprising at first. It's natural to expect that the physical ability and mental attitudes of the Bengalis would draw them towards softness, grace and beauty. But those who know the Bengalis closely and have studied their nature, are aware that this oxymoronic self-contradiction is peculiar to them. Floral softness and thunderous hardness entwine in their character. So, as widespread is the ignominious disrepute of their cowardice as is their distinction in extreme bravery.

The struggles and clashes of the national movement in India today have become pervasive; it has spread widely and its momentum ranges from the mountains to the sea. Common people of all the provinces, irrespective of cast and creed, have joined in this long struggle of establishing self rule. The Marathis, the Madrassis, the Gujratis, the Parsees, the Biharis—they are all in this struggle. They fill the ranks of the prisons, suffer persecutions. But in the indomitable desire for freedom, it is the Bengalis who have exercised great spells of fire, in paying a price and repaying the debt of the motherland, by pledging their lives. Where else in India have schoolboys welcomed the punishment of death by hanging, have women fired pistols and grey-haired mothers, who had never stepped out of their home, taken bullets into their chests?

The Kali temple on Reading Road, established by the combined efforts and contributions, confers on the Bengali community of New Delhi, a right to feel proud. That the Bengalis with their troublesome and self-defeating logic and work ethics only quarrel, engage in divisive politics, ruin institutions are regular complaints against them. Maybe these rumours are not entirely unfounded. Individual achievements of Bengalis are matchless. Their intellect, wisdom, and pursuit of perfection are accepted by one and all. One has to accept with profound regret that the Bengalis have not shown enough strength in setting up large institutions through the combined co-operative efforts of many. Therefore this Kali temple pleases the mind. Not built by the purse of any royal, nor with the solitary contribution of a rich person, this temple has been built entirely through the collected subscriptions of domiciled Bengalis and an icon of the goddess Kali has been consecrated inside.

Bengalis have come to this North Indian city to earn a living by serving in government offices. Some of them have earned profusely as members of the Executive Council, some have earned a limited pay as a general clerk. All of them have contributed, willingly and with respect. Funds for the temple was raised by degrees. I convey accolades to them. They are worthy, indeed.

He, who planned the temple, although unknown, is praiseworthy. It is free of adornments and ostentation, with a simple structure. Its flavour is not that of the business district of Burrabazar in Calcutta, nor does it have the ultramodern streamlines of an American style. A look at it from the distance is pleasing to the eyes and going near it fills the mind with sanctity.

A few steps up there is a wide veranda, surrounded by a low, reticulated wall. The temple is in the middle and around it is a pathway. Visitors circumambulate the icon in the temple along that path, ring the bell hanging at the temple door before touching the hallowed dust to their heads. Devotees pray to the goddess about their deepest desires. Natural light and fresh air face no hindrance to enter the temple. It is not dark inside the temple, nor is the air dank and unclean with stale piled-up flowers and Ganges water.

The courtyard of the temple is amply wide. On one side is the ridge of the Aravalli mountains. Erect and high stone walls have been put together by cement. On the other side is the street and the railings. At the back, in a corner, is the residence of the temple priest. A small residential quarter was built there by the temple trust.

In a distant land it is not easy to find a priest to carry out the daily rituals of the goddess. To bring a suitable person from Bengal requires a regular income for him and an assurance to maintain his family. So the temple trust has fixed a monthly stipend for the priest. This has grades, increments and leave rules. He gets a fixed share of the donations of the visitors. In this era, he who serves the god has to abide by the fundamental rules of professional service.

When the lives of men had not become complex, his needs were limited and wants were paltry, then the Brahmins hardly needed riches. He gave lessons to students, bestowed knowledge to disciples, worshipped and meditated, unperturbed. He was sans greed, unattached, clean, pure and *sattvik.* Those days are no more, no more are those Brahmins. The priest's daily needs have also grown within his family life. His wife needs innerwear, children need baby food and daughter requires cosmetics. Dealing with this mortal life's family, society and surroundings with indifference and having in mind only the welfare of his clients in the afterlife, is sure to quicken the pace of the onset of one's own afterlife. So, the temple needs to have free accommodation for the temple priest, which has electric light, tap water and other ordinary comforts befitting the civil standards of a low income Bengali family.

I entered the temple, leaving my shoes by the steps. The priest generously offered me holy water sacralised at the feet of the goddess, flowers and bits of prasad.

In contrast to Calcutta, the presence of a Bengali man in a formal European suit in a temple is not derisive here. People here regard outfits in their functional roles, not as an introduction to one's mental framework. This has been possible due to the presence of diversely attired people in the city. Here, in this temple come Brahmins from Madras, the Singhs of Punjab, the bais of Maharashtra, widows from Bengal, to offer salutations. Their dresses, ornaments, manner of clothing are all different. They are the devotees, this is their only identity; and their clothes are only meant to cover their nudity and to save them from the heat and the cold.

An open field lay ahead of the temple. There, under a tarpaulin-covered temporary structure, Durga Puja is held in autumn with great élan. An exhibition is held during that time, showcasing the handiwork of Bengali children. In the daytime, boys and girls get a share of the food offered to the deity and at night, youths of amateur theatre groups play female roles in dramatic renditions by shaving their moustaches and chiselling their voice to a fine feminine tone.

At the Kali temple, on every new moon night, devotional songs dedicated to the goddess are sung. Songs whose subjects are the goddess Shyama are sung there in a kirtan style by the main vocalist accompanied by a co-singer. Compositions are devotional in nature, melodies lack variety. They lack the appeal found in the renditions of great devotees and fall short in the emotional appeal of a worshipper's unique surrender in devotion. The items sung are mere interpolations from the point of view of music and futile imitations in the sphere of devotion. They fail summarily. Before the goddess Kali, the best offering is the kind of song sung in a devotee's own voice, like Ramprasad, 'I've made my heart a cremation ground, because a cremation ground is your favourite.'

In the course of these song-filled gatherings, the middle-aged gentleman with whom my acquaintance developed into a deep intimancy was Mohit Kumar Sengupta. He was over fifty, portly, of average height and worked in the Audits and Accounts Services. He has made a name in government circles as an efficient officer. At present he is posted as the Financial Adviser in the Transport Department. His pay and post are both important. The names of his other two brothers are well-known to college-goers in Bengal. There are few examinees in this decade who have not read *Economics* by M. Sen and *Civics* by Mihir Sen while preparing for examinations. Sengupta himself was well-known during his student days. He was the second student-editor of the Presidency College magazine. He is a widower, very affable and sufficiently honoured in the Bengali society of New Delhi. He closely involves himself in all the activities of the Bengalis. His appearance is a certainty in the musical gatherings of the Kali Temple.

What newspapers are to Fleet Street, tailors are to Savile Row. In that way, temples are to Reading Road in New Delhi; not one or two, three in a row. If the road is named Temple Street, it would be more just.

I guess that the Laxmi-Narayan temple built by Sri Jugal Kishore Birla stands out as the best man-made abode of the gods in this century. Not for its enormity alone, its neat architecture and the colossal expenditures lavished to build it have no known match. People gather here from all corners of the world to visit it; devotees of all faiths and creeds as well as tourists of European and American origins; film-spools of cameras run out photographing it round the clock from myriad angles.

It happened nearly twelve years ago that Jugal Kishore Birla wished to establish a Hindu temple, commemorating the name of his father, where all Hindus may have equal rights of entry. The Birlas hail from Jaipur, but the purpose of building a temple there with this specific ambition seemed limiting. How many visit Jaipur in a year? Therefore, the venue was fixed at Delhi, the capital city of India for millennia. Here, in Indraprastha, reigned kings of the Mahabharat era; dwelled Sanjukta and Prithviraj; Emperor Qutubuddin's seat was at Siri; Emperor Shah Jahan held the sceptre at the Red Fort. The open and wide meadows on the banks of the Yamuna, the forest lands of the Aravallis, the dusty streets of now-lost towns and settlements, have all mingled in one body as through the ages have the Sakas, the Huns, the Mughals, the Afghans. In the future India too, Delhi will be the central jewel in the garland of Indian cities. It's certain that Wardha won't be the capital city of independent India.

The construction work of the temple started in 1932. Many engineers, numerous workers, hundreds of masons and an assorted workforce laboured hard for six years continuously. The temple, commemorating the name of Baldeo Das Birla, father of the mega-rich Birla brothers, was completed in 1938 and was consecrated for worshipping Laxmi and Narayan.

The style of the temple is a good example of Indian architecture. The red stone steeples with saffron edges resemble a piece of red cloth with a saffron border. A flight of vast wide marble stairs ascend from the main road to the temple. On the floor and walls are colourful depictions of flowers and motifs made by arranging variously hued pieces of stones. Numerous fresco paintings decorate the bulwark. These are the works of artists from the Jaipur Art College. The subject matter and craftsmanship deserve to be praised. The Principal of Jaipur Art College is a Bengali, Koshal Mukherjee. He is a contemporary of Nandalal, Asit Kumar, Samar Gupta, the doyens of the Renaissance of modern art in Bengal. A reason to feel glad is that a Bengali architect has made a significant contribution in the planning of this temple.

Within the temple, the deities are crafted of white marble. Flowers offered by innumerable visitors cover the feet of the deity and the inner sanctum. Through a slit on the iron chest at the door, visitors insert coins as donation. Towards the left of the temple is a large dharamshala, a guest house built in memory of the mothers of the Birla clan. Adjacent to it is an open auditorium. Tuneful singers render devotional songs there each evening. An audience of more than a thousand might sit there. This is made audible to the people outside through a microphone. I could hear the refrain of the song from a distance, long before reaching the temple, 'Lord Ramachandra, I pray to thee, by your grace rid me of my severe fear of this world.'

A large park has come up at the back of the temple. It's a later-day development. A number of objects in the park might entertain visitors. There is a large white elephant spouting water through its trunk like a fountain; a crocodile is there which emits water through its mouth. Fountains, flower-beds, artificial streams, tunnels etc. in the park pull to it the young ones and the visiting villagers in hordes. They throng there each afternoon. Some occupy the bench, some sit on the swing, some stroll around. Seth Jugal Kishore was not parsimonious. The estimated cost of the park and the temple at pre-war prices is approximately twenty lakh rupees.

There is a trust comprising three members of the Birla family, three representatives of the Arya Representative Association of Punjab and three from the local Sanatan Dharmasabha. The trust maintains the temple and the adjacent park, guest house, etc. The system of managing is modern. Representatives are elected every three years. In such minor affairs too there is a stamp of modernity.

The shoe-room, fitted with racks, by the staircase before entering the temple is rather nice. Shoes are kept there in lieu of numbered cardboard tokens to prevent a possible interchange of high-heeled ladies' shoes with Kabuli slippers. Depositing the token, the exact pair is returned, as is in the case of one's hat, brolly or stick in Savoy, Grosvenor or the Great Eastern.

Mahatma Gandhi had inaugurated this temple. There was no one better fitted for this function. Who else would open the gates of a temple that confers equal access to the Brahmins, Sudras and Harijans? The name of the finest human soul of this era has remained united forever with the most beautiful twentieth century Indian temple.

The third temple on land adjacent to the Birla temple was built mainly with the financial support of the Birlas. This belongs to the Buddhists. The location and the style of this small temple, situated midway between the Kali temple built by the Bengali community and Laxmi-Narayan temple, cannot be ignored. The solemnly meditating image of Lord Tathagata is in the temple. There are also a few yellow-robed Buddhist monks. One of them was an ardent admirer of the poet Rabindranath. In memory of the poet, he planted a bakul (*Mimusoaps elengi*) tree in the temple-yard. A Bengali historian presided over the ceremony of planting the 'Rabi-bakul' tree. He is Dr Surendra Nath Sen, the Keeper of Imperial Records of the Government of India.

Sri Sen was an Associate Professor in the Calcutta University. The value of his erudite research on the history of Maharashtra is well-acknowledged among historians. Sri Sen stands out among those few servants of the Bengal edifice who devote their time to literature, even after leading an easy life with a fat pay from the government and who, among the historians, chooses to write history in Bengali, even after receiving degrees from the University of Oxford. He hails from the district of Barisal. His manner of speaking has the unique accent of those parts.

On one side of Reading Road are the temples and on the other are quarters. Those are the residences of clerks and similar staff in government offices. Long-stretched barracks, some are shaped like letter 'L' and some are like letter 'E', without the bar in the middle. A patch of grassy grounds lie in front. The temples and the quarters—such juxtaposition of the lovely and the ugly are rarely seen elsewhere. Each of the barracks houses nearly two score families. These are affordable arrangements by the government for people with lower salaries. This is the East End of New Delhi.

Although the appearance is not too good, living comfort is not low in these quarters. It is particularly so if judged from the point of view of its price. It costs only one-tenth of the salary as rent. The office takes care to deduct it from a month's pay. The lowest salary of the Secretariat employees is sixty rupees. So, the rent is six rupees. This has two bedrooms, one kitchen, one store, a slice of an inner courtyard and a small veranda outside.

There are water taps, bathrooms, electric lights and hold your breath, a large ceiling fan. Enough light, enough air and enough dust has free passage through it. In Calcutta, the chance of obtaining this sort of accommodation at this price is one in ten millions.

Not only accommodation, there is furniture too. Like a bride adorned with ornaments in a wedding, a government quarter is available with furniture provided by the central PWD. Two cots, one closet, one table and three chairs are available at a monthly rental of two rupees.

A barrack with the compound in front makes a Square. Most are named after founders of the British Empire in India. Clive Square is named after the English gentleman who laid the foundation of British Empire in the mango grove at Plassey. He arrived in India as an insignificant clerk of the East India Company at an annual salary of eighty rupees and returned as the richest man in England. Robert Clive arrived in the Madras port in 1744, an unknown destitute and when he returned to England as the Chief of the Army, alighting at Portsmouth in England from a ship, remarks entered on him in the Annual Registrar of England were, 'This Colonel possesses cash worth rupees twenty million, his wife's casket contain jewels worth rupees two hundred thousand.

None other in England, Scotland and Ireland has more money than him.'

A 'Square' has been named after Lord Dalhousie, who added Punjab and Burma to the British Indian Empire, per force occupied Satara from the Peshwas, snatched away Jhansi, Nagpur, Berar belonging to the Nizam and seized Ayodhya from Nawab Wajed Ali Shah.

Yet another Square perpetuates the name of Warren Hastings, who looted a king's ransom from Chet Singh, the king of Kashi; gathered at least fifteen millions worth of cash and jewels by persecuting the Begums in Ayodhya. His long list of evils were exposed to the world through an unforeseen oratory by Edmund Burke in the Parliament of England at the time of his impeachment. A number of English female visitors passed out in the gallery of the parliament, hearing the hair-raising annals of his sinister acts.

And then there are the names of English army chiefs of various ranks who fought to quell the Sepoy Mutiny—Havelock Square, Outram Square, Wilson Square, Nicholson Square and so on. Only the name of Major General Hewitt is missing from the naming of the Squares, who, on 9 May 1857, at Meerut garrison, abused and humiliated eighty-five Indian sepoys, after putting their hands and feet in irons, in front of the entire brigade present. Indian sepoys helplessly watched that day the ignominy of their comrades. Their mouths were shut but eyes spit fire. That fire was not extinguished easily.

The next day was a Sunday. Crepuscular darkness foreshadowing the approaching night had descended over the garrison at Meerut. The British soldiers were all set to attend service in church. What were the Indian soldiers at, then? Perhaps they were resting. Just then reports of gunfire filled the air!

Sepoys of the infantry had turned their weapons on to the British commanders. They were pulling the triggers. Booms rent the sky, the air, the walls and the meadows. It was the beginning of the Sepoy Mutiny in the North.

Although it failed owing to a lack of leadership, unorganised ways, unplanned methods, lack of communication and not having a central command, one has to accept today that it was the very first enterprise to overthrow the British from India and to initiate self-rule.

The next morning, sepoys from Meerut reached Delhi on horseback. Badshah Bahadur Shah was then on the throne of Delhi. This old Mughal emperor's character had not an iota of Babur's valour, Akbar's personality or Aurangzeb's war-skills. He was too weak to utilise the sepoys' bravery, energy and arsenal. He failed miserably to deliver a triumphant ending to these anti-British mass revolts.

The width of Delhi was only seven miles. The residents were agitated. Forty thousand British-trained, armed-with-British-weaponry, skilled-in-war sepoys guarded it. Fourteen large cannons were strategically placed over the fortification. The largest ammunition store was within the fort. In addition, there were sixty smaller cannons. There were many skilful artillery men, most of whom had been part of the British army a few days ago. They were well-trained in European combat methods and were disciplined. Indian engineers who strengthened the Delhi fort had received their training in latest methods from the British army. There was scarcely any hope to capture Delhi in the minds of the assembled British force at the ridge. Not even the slightest reasonable chance of the fort falling was there.

But still the sepoys lost the battle. The English captured Delhi. Islamic rule over India came to an end. Union Jack was unfurled over the Red Fort which had been built by Emperor Shah Jahan, a hundred years ago.

There was an army contingent of a little over fourteen thousand in the garrison at the ridge, situated at the end of the town. Not all of them were European. Nearly five and a half thousand among them were Indian sepoys. Add to it, another two and a half thousand sepoys—Indian, of course—who were sent by the princely states under the suzerainty of the British crown. Those princes, in return, now enjoy a statutory provision of twenty-one, eleven, seven or five gun salutes.

The British army hit the Grand Trunk Road from Karnal and garrisoned at the ridge, where now stands the Delhi University. Many battles were fought over a long time in the present-day Subzi Mandi by the defending sepoys. Afterwards, the old Vice-Regal Lodge was built in place of that makeshift abode of British soldiers at the ridge. Now, students sit there to take down notes on physics, chemistry or economics. In a house, a little way from there, Mahatma Gandhi sat on a fast for three weeks in 1924 in protest against the communal violence in Delhi. In an effort to unify all parties and creeds, Pandit Malaviya convened a meeting there for the first time.

The English had made out that unless Delhi was captured without delay the British Empire in India would be lost forever. To them, to win was to become a Badshah and to lose was to be a pauper. So they risked everything to be the victor. Brigadier Archdale Wilson was then the commander of the British camp. He was, however, not very hopeful of a win.

The summer passed, the rains were over and the first half of autumn also was almost through. More than half the British soldiers were down with fever, dysentery and other afflictions. Captain Lawrence was unrelentingly sending anxious messages from Punjab, How long? How long a wait to win Delhi? Only in the Punjab were the sepoys still loyal; the garrison at Ambala had not raised any discontent. But not much longer would all be peaceful. It's Delhi, Delhi and Delhi alone on which rests the fate of John Company in India.

By the beginning of September that year, at last sufficient ammunition and fire-arms reached at the garrison at the ridge on elephant back from Firozpore. British infantry captains gained back their hope and courage. John Nicholson superseded Brigadier Wilson to command the battle.

It was the fourteenth of September. Night was almost over, but a trace of light was yet to appear on the eastern horizon. The English forces invaded Delhi fort. As a precursor to the main invasion, the fortification was bombarded with cannonballs continuously all day and night for last six days. Towards the Kashmiri Gate, the British soldiers made incursions in groups. The windowpanes of houses in far distant places quaked with the roars of cannon-firing. The wide early-dawn skies became tinged with the scarlet hints of raining fireballs, like the vermilion-hued parting of a a married woman's hair.

This tooth-and-nail battle continued for hours. At last, the bolted entrance of Kashmiri Gate fell to the ground with a huge, thundering bang.

A small detachment of the Engineering Division had snaked their way up the fort wall. They detonated explosives to raze the heavy-built, impenetrable Kashmiri Gate to the ground. With these men's supra-human courage, the English snatched victory for themselves. The English historians have admitted that eight of them were Indians.

Emboldened by the victory, the British forces gushed through the fallen gateway into the fort. They assaulted the opponents with doubled ferocity. With an open sword in hand, Nicholson conducted his soldiers. A sepoy trained his gun at him. In a moment Nicholson fell to ground with a cry. The bullet had struck him on the forehead. The vanquished old monarch Bahadur Shah fled from the fort. He concealed himself in the edifice of Humayan's tomb, four mile south of the Red Fort. He took refuge with a Muslim fakir there. People say he was betrayed by the fakir who turned him over to the hands of a young officer in the espionage service of the English, named Hudson.

'Hama aaj daste gayer nala kunand,
Shadi, aaj daste, khestan fariyad.'

(When one's own hand ends up slapping one's own face, then, dear Shadi, why feel wretched in the prospect of maltreatment of others).

The captured monarch was brought to Delhi in a palanquin. He was put on trial there. He was awarded the punishment of exile for life to Burma. He breathed his last there under confinement after five years. Poor, ill-fated Bahadur Shah, the last Islamic monarch of India!

The next day, from the same place in Humayun's tomb, Hudson captured three more fugitives. They were the two sons and a grandson of Bahadur Shah. They offered themselves to be in custody. They were given the assurance that they would also be tried like Bahadur Shah.

Hudson brought them to Delhi on a horse-drawn carriage. Hudson pulled over the carriage to a stop near Delhi Gate. He took the gun out himself and then in succession pulled the trigger right at the centre of the bosoms of the three captives. Royal blood spilled over in torrent on the dusty streets of Delhi. The dead bodies were kept for three days in the open field at Chandni Chowk as public exhibits. Passers by silently wiped their tearful eyes again and again at the sight of the decomposed cadavers of the scions of the Emperor's family.

Seven

In our Puranas and history, instances of chaste wives, devoted sons and younger siblings brimming with fraternal love and loyal servants can be found. The entire populace of the land are aware of Sita, the daughter of King Janak, Ramachandra, the son of King Dasaratha, Laxman, the son of Sumitra and Hanuman, the follower of Rama. But if one desires to know the example of a husband devoted to his wife, first of all he should pay a visit to Priyanathbabu, husband of Indumati Roy, my maternal aunt's close friend.

Sri Priyanath Roy, circumrotates about the tender pedestal of Indumati. If one were to go by her pre-marriage bio-data, Indumati's maiden surname was Dasgupta. She did her English honours in Gokhale College, learnt playing the sitar in Sangeet Sammilani. During the Brahma Samaj prayer on the occasion of Maghotsab, she, in a full-sleeve blouse, would sing, 'Lord, you are our father'. One of her elder brothers is an officer in the railways, another is a barrister.

Indumati's father had bullion in the iron-chest, but she lacked beauty in her form. Ergo, after waiting futilely over some time for a prospective ICS, or Europe-returned, or a deputy etc. groom, she entered into the arms of Priyanathbabu in the auspicious month of *Magha* on the fifth lunar day of the bright-phase of the moon at the fag end of youth. Following marriage, the bride's surname changed and the groom's position in office improved. He became a superintendent from an assistant. It proved beyond doubt that Indumati had brought good fortune with her!

Priyanathbabu, of course, is the *nath* (i.e. husband) to his wife; may be *priya* (favourite) too. It should be so, at least. But, if you ask me.... However, let that go. Not that I'm about to choose him as a groom for my daughter!

Priyanathbabu resides in a B-type quarter on Mahadeo Road. Every item, from eggs to living quarters, is graded in New Delhi —A, B, C, D, etc. Diamonds are judged on brightness, muslins on their fineness. Government employees are graded on the basis of their salaries. In the PWD account, quarters are grouped according to pay. 'A' type quarters are for those who receive five to six hundred rupees, 'B' type, for those who earn four to five hundred a month. Those who earn above six hundred are entitled to a bungalow. This too is bound by rules. Not only in denominations of amenities or build, but also with respect to its location. The postal address of an occupant suggests his quantum of pay. Residents of Hastings Road earn three to four thousand and those of Tughlaq Road, less than that. Unless one earns more than one thousand rupees, he would not get a bungalow at Raisina Road.

I was matching house-numbers, looking for the house. Finally, at the destination, in a room by the veranda, a servant in a half-clean vest, an electric iron in hand, was tending a chocolate coloured Benarasi sari. 'Is this Priyanathbabu's?' I asked.

'Yes. This is Mr Roy's.'

The frown on the forehead and strain in the voice clearly conveyed displeasure in the suffix 'babu'. So I corrected myself.

'Will you send for Mr Roy?'

'I am Mr Roy.'

God save the King! How was I to anticipate that the husband of Mrs Indumati Roy would be busy ironing a sari at half past eight in the morning? But I'd burnt my bridges. Consequently, I was compelled to brief him about me and explain the nature of the relation between his wife and my maternal aunt. Mr Roy went in and picked up necessary directions to call me into the drawing room to sit. He assured me, reverentially alluding to her, that she was taking a bath and wouldn't be long.

A small carpet, of Mirzapuri make, was spread on the canvas-covered floor of the drawing room. A Japanese vase, albeit without flowers, stood on a tripod. A folded canvas easy-chair occupied a corner. The region where the head rubs against the canvas had been soiled by the well-oiled hairdo of those who sat there. A couple of glass-framed samples of needlework hung on the wall. For fear of any possibilility of confusion regarding the identity of the artist in the mind of the viewers, the name 'Indu' was inscribed in large letters at the corner of the works on display. One of these depicted a basket with a few roses in it. Another is a mongrel of many hues. Rampant use of red, blue, green, yellow might well have earned it the name, Vibgyor. Above the head of the mongrel was written in English, 'God is good.' It convinced us that the house-mistress was a pious lady. But, why she chose a dog to underline it was not clear. I guess it was a textual error. It should have been 'Dog is good.'

Small talk with Priyanathbabu occupied me for a while. I listened, while he held forth, almost exclusively, on his revered better half. That she needed a hot cup of tea in bed, that she took pains to measure out daily provisions to the cook, that she forbade the entry of any cooked item from the market inside the house, that it was she who did all the sundry work at New Delhi's 'Bengal Women's Association', that Lady Mitra couldn't do without her at all and so forth.

Indumati Roy entered; Mr Roy stood up. This was in accordance to English manners.

The mistress of the house, Mrs Roy, took her seat. She began a detailed description of the paucity of space in her house. She was hopeful that a bungalow on Gurudwara Road would be available in six months' time. She felt constrained in this house; she was unable to do up the rooms to her liking. It was true that much of the furniture she brought from Simla was yet to be unpacked—she had returned from Simla only five months ago. She did the Delhi–Simla back and forth at least once each year. This was her first encounter with summer in Delhi. But the sojourn in the summer capital of the Government of India had to be abandoned this year. She was told that the new commander-in-chief had said that the prospect of victory in the war would be affected if the capital was moved to Simla. What nonsense! Whatever happened, if it became any hotter, no matter what one said, she would 'have to' go to Simla!

Did I know the recent whereabouts of 'Baby', her pal and my maternal aunt? Was her daughter's marriage settled? In which class was her son studying? She said her own time to write letters was scant. She has so many things to attend to all the time! For example, that very afternoon, at 4 pm she had a party. She stopped and directed her attention to Priyanathbabu, 'Has my sari for the occasion been ironed?'

Looking at my watch, I sought to take leave.

Why leave so early? Oh, I see, certainly the hour is late. How long are you here? Where will you go from Delhi? What happened in the Continent? Unless the war is over you can't return. Were you in London when there was 'bomming'? How is life out there? Do you get to buy 'Drin' shampoos? 'Tangi' lipsticks? Poor me, those are very scarce here! Gosh, you've not taken tea or anything here! He (Mr Roy) is getting late for office. Well, do visit another time and have something here.

I'd been asked to visit one more person. The address was not known to me. I enquired of Priyanathbabu, sorry, Mr Roy, 'Could you tell me where V.R. Venkateshwaran's residence is? In which department is he an assistant secretary?'

The expression 'violent explosion' often appears these days in newspapers. I didn't quite know exactly what it meant though Priyanath Roy's state helped me gather its connotations.

'Assistant secretary! Venkateshwaran said it to you? Airs, it's all airs. This Madrassi dwells on pretence alone. He thought you are new here and would not get at the truth. Assistant secretary, pooh! One who gets that post a year or two before retirement, he is lucky indeed. Now it is wartime. That's why even second division clerks are getting to be superintendents. Otherwise, one has to grey one's hair before becoming an assistant. At the time I became the superintendent, Woodhead sahib, Sir John Woodhead, who was later raised to the rank of the lieutenant governor of Bengal was the deputy secretary. He called me and said, 'Roy, a man who can work like you...'

I felt repentant. This was a ripe example of becoming the cause of someone else's heart-ache, completely unawares.

Venkateshwaran has a home but no home-maker. Had she been there though, she would have invited trouble for herself. Were she of antiquated habits, she would have hung herself; were she modern-minded, she would have eloped with her husband's friend, only to be an actress in the Bengali movies afterwards. A wife may live with a drunkard husband, or bandy words with a husband on his inamoratas. But to be the wife of an indifferent person is the worst. Love is good, hatred is unfortunate, but the most killing of all is indifference—it neither attracts, nor repels—only remains forgetful.

Devotees say that unless one's pursuits—knowledge and constant meditation—are directed towards god, the bliss of meeting god does not occur. Varadarajalu Venkateshwaran was not eager to attain god. But he served the Secretariat with the focussed attention of a devotee.

All that mattered to him was office, office and only, office. It was only work and work and work.

He sat at his table at half past nine, soon after the sweeper finished cleaning the premises. Afternoons rolled into evening darkness; the employees, ranked above and below him, left for the day for their homes; other colleagues departed one by one. Venkateshwaran continued working all alone, single-mindedly. He returned home at 8:00 pm or even later in the night. It was always the same, all through the seasons. He was never on leave, never absent. Often on Sunday, at mid-day, he paid a visit to the office. He sat down with his files, made notes in them, underlining pages with flag marks: 'Fresh Receipt' or 'PuC–Paper under Consideration'. Friends tease him, 'Venkat knew only how to labour, when will he enjoy life?'

Venkateshwaran only smiled at the suggestion and swung his head to and fro. Maybe, he says to himself, 'What nonsense! Whatt-ta foool-la! Enjoy? Huh, from third-division to second-division clerk, then assistant, to superintendent and from superintendent to assistant secretary: a real long distance to bridge. Enough of life is left for enjoying. Before that, one needs promotions, needs raises. Oh my job, my dearest job, you are my presiding deity, the Shyam to my Radha!'

A younger brother of Venkateshwaran was in England. His objective was breaking into the ranks of ICS. I knew him from there. I observed in him the same devotion that his brother had. I hope, one day his name would be proudly printed in the Civil servants' list.

The people from Venkateshwaran's native place are well established in New Delhi. At the outset, all the departments of the Government of India were in Calcutta. The building, near Laldighi, where at present the governor of Bengal resides, was the official residence of governor-generals ranging from Warren Hastings to Lord Hardinge. At that time, many Bengalis worked in the Secretariat. Later, the capital was moved to Delhi. Their numbers dwindled and people from other provinces started joining their ranks, which have grown over the years. They are now occupying higher echelons in the service. The Madrassis are foremost in the race for chair. They work hard, speak little and shirk their duty very rarely.

The Madrassis have their club, association and school in New Delhi. They have boarding houses too. In it there are small tables akin to desks found in schools. On these tables, food is served on a banana leaf. Only for four annas, one gets *swathama, kuttu, sambhar* and *appalama*. These comprise the regular diet of anyone from Tamil Nadu or Andhra. Sometimes they serve *taiyar-patchatti* with the regular menu, which is curd mixed with shredded pieces of coconut. It is a feast that day!

They are frugal not only in their food habits but also in their choice of clothing. A sheet of cloth, divided into two, constitutes their outfit along with an ordinary loose shirt that covers their torso. A small towel is placed on the shoulder. A pair of ordinary sandals adorn their feet. That's all. They go everywhere, but the office, in this outfit with no sense of self-consciousness. Whatever they might do, the Madrassis never bewail their clothes!

The apparel of their women is also shorn of excesses. The ornaments they wear are few in number. In count, of course, not in value. Even an ordinary housewife might wear a pair of diamond ear-rings on her ear. Its price may well send many a Bengali husband into shock. Though most of the young girls seem to lack a great deal of charm in their looks, they possess elegance. It is as though the entrance to their homes receives a coat of ornate paints each dusk and dawn as they bedeck their braids and chignons with fresh flowers. In most cases, their accomplishments include music.

I was invited to dine in the house of a new acquaintance, a Madrassi gentleman. He is a high official and receives a salary of two thousand. The menu for dinner however ended up moistening my eyes rather than my tongue. But his wife was an expert Veena player. She played that stringed instrument so beautifully that though my stomach was not filled, my ears were filled to satiety. It helped me take a liberal view of the thrifty menu!

In this, the Punjabis differ from the Madrassis. In habits and manners, the Punjabis are more than modern, they are ultra-modern. The young and the old, seem to be, in one spirit, fiercely emulating the Europeans. Had it been the boys only, it would have perhaps been okay. But the girls are also a part of this trend.

The races, clubs and carnivals–the three godheads of the ultra-moderns–are most frequented and championed by Punjabi women! They may toss down four rounds of sherry playfully, dance foxtrot untiringly till the wee hours of the morning. On their forms, it is an excess that overtakes grace. Before their weddings, they are willowy but later on, bloated. They are fair-complexioned, but their countenance lacks tenderness. They are known to go to the extent of thrashing their servants and maids, using their own hands, in order to 'tame' them. The daughters of Punjab are not soft, in mind or in body.

The European school of thought was first unveiled in Bengal. Bengalis welcomed the English culture and system of education. The Bengalis of that era possessed profuse energy and had matching genius. They did not merely swallow the literature, science and civilisation of the English, but they assimilated them. They metabolised them after digesting them with the juices of their own cultural heritage. It was not sheer borrowing of occidental thought; it was bearing of that idealism. The result of this was manifested through Michael Madhusudan, Vivekananda and C.R. Das, among others. In literature, arts and fine arts, an era of Renaissance came about in Bengal; this brought with it a brand new impetus to patriotism. It taught fearlessness to the youth, infused self-awareness among women. At that acme of history, the iconic Mother Bengal won her seat in the hearts of all Indians.

Punjab came in contact with Europe at the very end. After one and a half century of establishing hegemony over Bengal by the British, Lord Dalhousie occupied Punjab. Nonetheless, Punjab could not internalise European culture, only mimicked its external features. Her contribution to India in literature, music and science is yet to flower. Her service to the nation is not yet enviable. In today's modern India, she is visible in bands of PWD engineers, subedars in the army and as IMS physicians. Till date, none other than Lajpat Rai from Punjab has been a president of the Congress.

The water of Laldighi in Calcutta is not red and the shape of Goldighi is quadrangular. But the name of Gol-market in Delhi is not a misnomer. It's round in shape and is located like an island, at the confluence of four roads. It is two-storied; there are tailoring shops upstairs while vegetables, fruits and non-veg. items are on the ground floor. All are sold in separate cells. Items available in the cells are indicated in English. The entry doors are covered with a fine net. A spring arrangement closes the door automatically. In the cell for fishes, a high cement platform, where fishes are kept, is fitted out with perforated water-pipes. Water drips continuously through the holes in the pipe. This automatically washes the platform. Fish are stored in the ice chest, all neat and clean, no pestering flies and there's hardly a chance of soiling the clothes of customers by an unfortunate spattering of muddy water. On either side of the market are stationery, grocery and sweetmeat shops. A few of these belong to Bengali shop keepers; the owner of one of such store sells curd, *sandesh* and other sundry Bengali sweets and savouries.

On way to Gol-market is Lady Hardinge college, the only all-women medical college in India. Among the students are Anglo-Indians, Madrassis, Marathis and Assamese; but no Bengalis. The sister-in-law of a Punjabi friend of mine, a professor, reads in fourth year here. She is pretty to look at. One comes across pretty faces in colleges and universities outside Bengal. To be deficient in prettiness is not the chief cause of motivation for higher studies in women there; neither is it regarded as a stop-gap solution before marriage.

The girl is meritorious; she stood first in her class in the college examinations. She said that her interest was more in surgery than in medicine. She will be a surgeon after passing out. Woe me, I'm undone!

Ladies of yore wielded brooms in their hands. They facilitated the flow of family life through its impartial application from floors to the posteriors of unruly husbands. Vanity bags have now replaced brooms in the hands of the modern ladies. Cosmetics and make-up stored within its interior infuses terror in their husbands' hearts and flutter in the hearts of others' husbands! If the ultra-moderns now begin to wield forceps in their hands then poor men would have to form an association of self-protection.

The young lady has quite a sense of humour. She bubbled over in laughter.

Though no Bengali student is enrolled in Lady Hardinge, a Bengali lady professor is there. Her one brother is an ICS, another is an IMS and two others are in higher echelons of the Accounts Service. Her sister is an artist. She is the art editor of the monthly magazine of the Government of India on industry and science, *Journal of Scientific and Industrial Research*. Other siblings are also well-established. She herself is a WMS which is akin to the ladies wing of the IMS. She receives a fat pay, earns enough by practising, behaves gently, speaks mildly and shows cordiality. She does not smack of 'Her physician ladyship'! Her government quarters are adjacent to the college premises. Her decent taste is apparent in its decor.

There are a number of lady physicians in New Delhi. A couple of them are from the United Provinces. The principal of Lady Hardinge college is from South India. Another one is from Punjab. Her father, Dharam Veer, is well-known in Punjab and her mother is European. Both of them are intimate friends of Subhas

Chandra Bose. She is married to a Bengali physician. It's better to be a physician couple than a school teacher or political activist couple. Political economy's concept of the division of labour extends to conjugal life also. In this division, the wives are speakers and husbands are listeners. If both are speakers, it causes serious ailments in domestic health.

Connaught Place might be called the Chowringhee of New Delhi. Most of the shops and stores there, are European or of a European fashion. Clothing or tailoring stores specialising in suit-making; photography studios; provision stores; beauty parlours to curl and perm hair; posh hotels serving lunch and movie theatres, they are all there in Connaught Place. Besides being a Chowringhee, this is also Clive Street. Most of the banks and offices are here. To buy patent stones of Bird Co., tiles from Martin's, or cement from Dalmia, one would have to hunt in Connaught Place.

Connaught Place was named after the late Duke of Connaught, the uncle of King George V. He visited India to formally inaugurate the present Indian Parliament, which was established consequent on the Montagu-Chelmsford Reforms. The memory of Indians was still fresh from the cruel manslaughter at Jallianwala Bagh. The elderly Duke made a reference to that in his inaugural speech; his tone was conciliatory, 'There occurred many errors and mistakes on either side. No use today to review those. Let us all forget the past and forgive each other. Forgive and forget.'

But the deal of 'forget-ness' works only among equals.Its stability between the ruler and the ruled is as instantaneous as is a water droplet on a lotus leaf. Time and again, at all moments, renewing the remembrance of the forgotten is effected by one side's brandishing of power and the other side's helpless howling in vain. It keeps happening. The Jallianwala Bagh is scarcely forgotten before Hijli occurs; before Hijli is consigned to oblivion, occurs a Contai or a Tamluk.

Connaught place is round in shape. A row of shops, facing the inside of the circle. Encircling this is another similar arcade which faces outward. Its name is Connaught Circus. A long veranda stretches under arches and pillars in the Roman style. In the afternoon, well-dressed men and women throng there, connoisseurs and refined buyers make their purchase; curious onlookers get a glimpse of fancy items on display in brightly-lit showcases.

Right adjacent to the veranda runs the wide main road. The zone marked out in white in the middle of the road indicates a parking place for waiting *tonga*s and motorcars. Traffic flows along either side of it. Across the road is a large park. An iron chain separates it from the pavement. This has benches for rest-seekers, a grassy ground welcomes playful children and myriad flower-beds delights flower-lovers.

Bengal is oblivious to the value of grass; this is because grass grows densely below the feet on every ground, not walked over for a few days. It is difficult to revile a worthless person as 'worthy of eating grass' in Northern India. It's scarcer than rice. It needs an effort to produce grass in a land where the summer temperature rises to one hundred and thirteen degrees and the annual rainfall is only twenty inches. Each blade of grass in the Connaught Place of New Delhi is sowed and reared by hand. The quantity of care, water and money that are put in by the Horticulture Department to this end may well be the material of an inflammatory editorial article of a daily.

We Indians, the Bengalis in particular, are not conscious enough about flowers. It's anybody's guess whether flowers and moonshine have been used beyond being necessary elements of maiden poems in college magazines. Bengalis like to believe that they are an artistic race; arguing may create a dispute but available records fall short in support. In an ordinary, low-income English household one might still spot some flowers on the dining table or in the living room. But on the contrary, a bouquet of flowers is rarely seen in the households of even well-to-do Bengalis. Thus, it is not the question of means, but of taste. For most Bengali families, flowers are in demand twice in lives, on wedding nights and for the funeral.

In olden times, there was the practice of worshipping the presiding deity of a family. It required scented flowers. Most of the households then nurtured a few flowering plants. Modernity has done away with the presiding deity. If one has to worship, it is considered wiser now to worship lords of flesh and bone than of stone or metal. The result becomes convenient. So, bosses in offices, district magistrates and leaders in politics are the receivers of our devotion now. Drawing rooms have occupied the space of worshipping sanctums in our homes. But the vacant place of the native hibiscus, marigold, or nagakesara has not been filled by carnation, dahlia, or gladiolus. No chance prevails today that one might chance upon a modern Shakuntala, sprinkling water, hidden by trees and encircling female attendants, in a flower garden. To have an eyeful of her, Dushyanta of this era may prowl around the lighthouse, the cinema hall, or by the lakes at Dhakuria. One who has the habit to keep flowers at his home in Calcutta is truly an out-of-the-ordinary foppish dandy.

There is no dearth of flowers in this city. The wide grounds of the government bungalows on either side of the road are replete with flowering plants. While walking one finds a pleasing sight. In the circular parks that are found at every junction of four roads are carefully maintained beds of flowers. Over the wall of the post office, on the hospital ground, seasonal flowers bloom aplenty. Clumps of canna flowers are found in Connaught Place. What remains in the summer is suggestive of the richness of the carnival of flowers in winter.

The sky of New Delhi has the look of a renunciate, its air has the sigh of a penniless despondent and its soil has the hardness of a practising ascetic. Nonetheless, the rows of trees, planted with care on roadsides, have created a shadowy cover for travellers, the grass-covered grounds of its parks and squares seem to have spread out a length of inviting green fabric, its posies of myriad flowers have woven effulgent enchantment. The most sympathetic milieu for romantic duos exists in New Delhi. In the duskiness of early evening, walking side by side along its quiet, deserted, fragrant pathways, newlywed couples grow impassioned at heart; their voices turn mellow, dropping to a whisper, close to the ear, sweet nothings, sans any meaning or logic, sans any necessity. And in that lulled evening hour, when the lover brings his lips close to the beloved's lovely dangly earrings, it is not unusual for his lips to touch elsewhere, slightly distracted.

Eight

I was awakened at dawn by the loud shrieks of a girl. It happens daily. I dub it shrieking; the girl's mother says it is music. The girl is taking lessons in music.

I don't know who invented music and when. I believed, till recently, the inventor had no cruel intentions. But I no longer believe so.

The girl has no melody in her voice; instead, she possesses demonic powers. The latter is all the more dangerous. She practices music two hours daily, from 5:00 am to 7:00 am in the morning. It is fit to say, she wrestles with the seven octaves. The neighbours are still non-violent, not because of Gandhiji's lessons but owing to sheer helplessness. There are several retributions of a civil society. This is one.

Europe has taught us quite a few bad things. A difference of opinions exists on which, among these, is the worst. Physicians believe it is the syphilis, elders opine, free love and Gandhiji says, it is the industries. My opinion is that the most harmful import from Europe is the harmonium. Nothing rivals its capacity of inflicting unbearable pain over the nervous system. It's no wonder that Pandit Jawaharlal Nehru has remarked that often, in a public meeting, when someone has begun a welcome song by playing its notes on a harmonium, before the welcome note is read, an indomitable desire arises in him to jump into the crowd and kick-smash that musical instrument and shatter it into bits.

Inert substances have an advantage. Their ability to tolerate is limitless. They never rebel. Only something as inert as a harmonium is capable of emitting tunes in step with two hours of discordant howling daily, of the same line, in the same note, on a loop, for the last ten days, 'Oh darling, you'd left never to return'. I have no idea who that darling is. Whoever he is, I do sympathise. If I knew the girl, I would have said to her with clasped hands – 'My dear girl, he has left under the compulsion to save his own life. It's certain that he would not return unless the yelling ceases. However deep love is, the yearning for life, nay for one's hearing, runs deeper.'

The girl is not the offender; neither blaming her mother is of avail. She knows that her daughter has to be married off. The groom's side will test the musical ability of the prospective bride before selecting her. Accordingly, the girl needs to be trained. So, buy a harmonium, engage a music tutor and get the girl to flex her throat muscles tooth and nail!

In our land, the responsibility of being endowed with all virtues lies squarely on girls. Nubile daughters need to be scholarly, adept in the arts and crafts, self-composed and an ace in domestic sciences. Even she who has passed B.Sc.with honours in physics is required to acquire sewing skills that she might portray flowers on a carpet, the culinary knowhow of spicing up a no-gravy banana-flower curry by adding sautéed *bodi* (pulse nugget) to it; and during the bride selection episode, is asked to sit on a mat before the friends and relatives of the prospective husband, in a pose often seen in a familiar photograph of Mahatma Gandhi i.e. pushing the bellows of a harmonium and singing '...the one who roamed in my dreams...'.

Expectations from men are not substantial at the altar of marriage. The mothers of brides are happy to have the information of a physician-groom's income; they do not bother with details of his skills in sports, dramatics, or in delivering lectures. Boys should do only one thing. It's either studies, or football, or 'inquilab zindabad'. Girls are judged not on the basis of a single skill but on the whole. Their values lie first in their beauty, then in their studies, music, dancing, sewing and in most cases, in the measure of their father's bank balance.

In ancient times, princesses enjoyed the privilege of selecting their own husbands. Men had to take tests of heroism and strength. Men then practised hard in order to rise to the occasion and be garlanded by the princess on the *swayamvar* day. These days, brides are not hard to come by. To be a winner, suitors are no longer required to break Puranic cross-bows (*haradhanus*) or pierce the eye of the fish by aiming only through its reflection in water. A fixed salaried job now suffices. Today, the sons of kings and generals need not undertake rigorous tours to faraway lands in search of girls blessed with an incomparable fair complexion. Neither do they have to dive into a sea of milk in search of the monster's life-seed, hidden within the black bumblebee inside the silver casket; nor do they have to awaken the sleeping princess of the netherworld by touching the magic golden wand to her temple. With a label stuck on them of being an officer in a government department, they confidently bang on the wedding god's door with a swagger and declare—go on, find the band of the adroit, the clever and the tender. Get your bevy of Renuka Sens, Madhuri Rays, Dolly Dutts and Arundhati Chatterjis. Princesses of today, with their long decorated tresses, arrive at the altar of marriage ferried by ninety nuggets of gold and three rounds of furniture. They garland the groom with a wreath of currency-notes that come as the dowry and chant, 'As long as my heart is yours, your heart is mine.'

I have not yet caught a glimpse of my ear-drum-rupturing music aficionado. I've been told that her features are not entirely bereft of beauty. She is good at her studies too. That might be so, but she's still got to learn singing as well! We are her wretched neighbours; we have our ill portend, who might undo that?

Relieving a sigh, I turned on my side in an effort to catch some sleep. It was in vain. This time it's a card, not a song. A gentleman wants to see me. Printed on the card is: P.C. Samaddar, BA, Deputy Assistant Controller. The gentleman was due to pay a visit in the morning. I'd failed to gather that morning would mean half past six at dawn!

Hi there! *Namaskar.* Were you sleeping? Then I'm really at fault. As for me, Sir, I get up at 5:00 am sharp for a morning walk. I walk a mile or two along Barakhamba to Feroz Shah Road and then via Windsor Place and Queensway to my house. I'm fine, sir. My dyspepsia is under control now.

Tea? Well, maybe I'll take another cup. I've already had a cuppa though. Haven't you had a cup yet? Don't you leave bed before seven? Oh Sir, I envy you. No need to work ten to six in an office, no boss around to bother about! Moving about in high circles only! By the way, did you ask Nehru about that dearness allowance?

Here, 'Nehru' refers to B.K. Nehru, undersecretary to the Finance Department. He is related to Pandit Jawaharlal Nehru. He is an ICS and his bride is a foreigner, but both are truly attached to the cause of India.

I apologised to him. I'd forgotten. But he is not someone to give up in despair. Please keep it in mind today, he continued. I'm told that they may settle on 17.5 per cent. What really interests me is the permissible salary limit for it; rumours are doing the rounds that those with a salary of over five hundred rupees wouldn't get it. Well, sir, just consider the injustice! What's our guilt? Price rise has affected everyone—whether their salaries are below or above five hundred, no? He buys milk at one seer a rupee in place of six seers and so do I, isn't it, sir? Then why should we be left out in case of the dearness allowance? For all such injustices, I feel a strong hatred for the government. Is it for nothing that Gandhi Maharaj has called it a Satanic government?

I reminded the Gandhi admirer that Gandhiji wanted to restrict everyone's salary below five hundred rupees.

No, no, that is not fair. He is a great soul, his needs are different. He is a sage. A bit of goat milk would do for him. For others, it is not so. Take my example. You are like one of my own family, so I wouldn't hesitate to elaborate. I receive eight hundred rupees. After standard deductions of income tax and provident fund, my net pay is seven hundred thirteen rupees and five annas. At the end of each month, there is a shortfall. You cannot really save on any count. I have to maintain my car, marry off my daughter and send my son to the Continent. To put a limit at five hundred is not right. Unless the standard of living is enhanced, India will not be a developed country. Look at Europe and America! Well, why don't we drive out the sahibs! What do they do? Only sign papers! All the writing and elaboration is done by us. But if the salary is restricted to five hundred, then an orderly would get only eight annas as salary, no! What, it won't be so? They would receive more then? It baffles me, sir. The minds of you congressmen are known to you alone.

I had neither time nor patience to explain the mysteries of congressmen's mental faculties to him. So, to change the topic, I raised the issue of Cripps' Proposals. I found that he was no less enthusiastic on the issue. He asked, do you think something will come of it? If it does, we are saved! The English will then learn a lesson for life! Gosh, in olden days, were there real open-fisted sahibs! Truly, they were like one's father and mother. I had just entered the Secretariat. Our office-superintendent was Mahatapbabu–Mahatap Ghose, a resident of Khardah in Bengal. He was an old man of fifty-seven. His service book though showed forty-eight. Another seven years to go before he became eligible for pension. Almost blind in both the eyes, his hand quivered while writing. One day, he signed over the typed space of a note on a file. We were all very tense. He would not survive this time. Murray sahib–Sir Alexander Murray–was our departmental secretary then. He summoned Mahatapbabu and asked if his son had passed the matric examination. Even if not, no problem. He asked him to bring his son there for a job and advised Mahatapbabu to enjoy his well-earned rest after having worked so hard for so many years. And now, sir, I could not secure a job for my second brother-in-law, a graduate from Calcutta University, even after two years of efforts.

He fumed, not only over his failure to manage a job for his second brother-in-law, but also over the matters of his own promotion.

Unless we have Swaraj, there is no happiness in service any more, sir. Nowadays, the English buggers are favouring the Muslims more. It is really their time of day. Who is competent and who is not, is no longer of consideration if he has a fez over his head! Nowadays, many of those who occupy the officer's chair can't utter a single line in English correctly. One Mr Khan has joined our office as a Controller; he's a complete idiot. The other day he used 'r' twice in 'reference'. Last month, a Muslim superseded four of us to be the Deputy Chief. Will all these injustices run on indefinitely? The English are bound to be beaten. But yes, I ask, why wouldn't it be so? The Muslims have a sense of fellow-feeling. Their leaders are always fighting for the rights of service-holders and their promotions. For even a trifle, five Muslim members in the Assembly would raise five questions, 'Will the Hon'ble Member be pleased to state...' If you try to be tough to a Muslim orderly, immediately the ministers will intervene and ask you to explain. And what will our very own Hindus do? All are Congressmen. They only talk about high ideals: Swaraj, independence; complete independence. Alas and alack, if all the jobs and benefits are for others, what do we do with Swaraj? I speak frank and clear, sir. Our Congress leaders are incapable of comprehending practical politics! Therefore they are spending their lives only in jails.

Trying to stop the man or arguing with him was pointless. His upbringing in a typical mediocre Bengali ambience has led him to believe firmly that a service is the most indubitable support of life and a post in the Government, a greatly desired good fortune. All his ideas, concepts, thoughts and dreams centre around this job. It begins with the character roll and ends with the pension. And in between the start and the finish, there is the expanse punctuated by promotions.

The office hours were approaching. Samaddarbabu got up to leave. Allow me to leave, then. It is time for office. Moreover, today I have to send the arrear-statement for this month. I'll come another afternoon then. Oh, you are not home in the afternoons? Then, I'll come around in the morning. Bye for today. In that matter of the dearness allowance, kindly...

I was invited to attend a tea party that afternoon. The Press Club of New Delhi was hosting a tea party in honour of Sir Stafford Cripps. Cripps had been most generously invited to numerous lunches, dinners and teas. He accepted only the invitation of the Press Club. He remarked that he was very grateful to the Indian Press for the cordiality extended to him and as a gesture of his gratefulness, he was obliged to accept the invitation.

The tea party was arranged in the lawns of the South Block. The number of invitees—native and foreign journalists together—was around a hundred and fifty. A few women, naturally foreigners, were there. The President of the Press Club is a Bengali, Ushanath Sen. He was a colleague of Late K.C. Roy, the father figure among journalists in India and the founder of Associated Press. He is now a partner of the Associated Press and works as the Executive Secretary in its Delhi office. Aged over sixty, well-built, balding, sharp-nosed and with a brilliant gleam in his eyes. In his appearance, conversation and bearing is the mark of a strong personality. He is a bachelor. If ever there was an assembly of confirmed bachelors in New Delhi, he would be the unanimously elected permanent President?

A press meet was to follow the tea party. This has been billed as the largest press conference ever in New Delhi, according to the annals of its private and public records. Not an inch of space was available in the committee room of the South Block. In this conference, Cripps revealed, for the first time, his proposals for public dissemination. For over an hour and a half, he answered more than a hundred questions asked by the assembled journalists. His manner of speaking, his adroitness, his tireless enterprise, were able to win him accolades from all journalists. He displayed a sense of humour too. Once, in the middle he said, 'Wait!' Then he removed his coat, raised the sleeves of his shirt and said, 'Now, come!' The entire conference roared with laughter.

Sir Stafford is one of the most famous lawyers of Britain. The quantum of his annual income has aroused envious shock among many in the circle of legal practitioners. Barrister Cripps' extraordinary dexterity in advancing arguments was proved anew in the press conference.

All human beings have a limit to their fortitude though. Unfortunately, Cripps was compelled to remind this to journalists there. Responding to an impolite question, he replied, at long last, in a stiff voice, 'Gentlemen, I've extraordinary patience, but that too has come to an end. I am not willing to tolerate any impolite suggestions about Britain's legislature or cabinet of ministers.'

The Indian journalists, especially reporters, are intelligent, have various strengths and have no fewer achievements in store. But they lack a sense of place. That they are not politicians is something they often forget. Politics can't do without a press, but the press can do without politics, for instance the *Harijan*. Journalists of this country are not satisfied as first-class reporters only; they have aspirations to be first-class politicians too. So unsavoury situations occur too often. They are not to blame. This country has no faith in specialisation. Here, the physician who treats fevers, operates on boils and extracts teeth too, if the situation so warrants.

A division of opinion occurred among journalists, whether Cripps' proposals were acceptable or not. The entire import of the proposals is assigned to the future. According to hearsay, Gandhiji had on his first visit to Cripps, likened his proposals to a post-dated cheque. Some over-enthusiast reporter appended it with it his own remarks, 'on a crashing bank'. From one mouth to another, the addition also gained currency as Gandhiji's original remark. There are many other instances too, in our political history, of such distortions through inadvertence or by design.

That evening, my two friends took me to a club.

The most renowned club in New Delhi is IDG–Imperial Delhi Gymkhana. Judging by the going scale of the caste system, the club is a superior Brahmin! The rights of admission are severely restricted. Not by its expensiveness alone, but also through its written rules. Both the admission fee and the monthly subscriptions are heavy. Moreover, none but first-class government servants like the ICS, IP, or Audits and Accounts, have access to be a member of the IDG. Although such restrictions do not bar private physicians, journalists and barristers to be members, the Club authorities take all precautions at the time of admitting new members so that only the crème de la crème of society, the financial and social elites, gain admission as members.

The club has a tennis lawn, a swimming pool and a band of its own. It has its own laundry too. This is the only club in New Delhi with permanent residential arrangements. IDG is not only a place for games or gossiping, it is a complete club.

The number two is Chelmsford. Situated close to the Secretariat, at the junction of Raisina and Queen Victoria Road, this club is the most alive spot in town. First, its fees are not that exorbitant, second, its location is more advantageous and third, non-Indians are fewer. The rules for induction of new members are also not that stringent. Each year, an annual swimming competition is held in the swimming pool of Chelmsford. Dances are held on Tuesday nights; on winter nights, inside the club and on summer nights, in the open. The dance floor in the open is not wooden, it's cemented.

The fried chops of Chelmsford Club is a gourmet's delight like Calcutta's famed Baghbazar's *rosogolla*.

Ladies are not required to pay a separate subscription amount here. The proud wives of achiever-husbands join her male friends at the card-table. With an ace partner, she sits dummy. Otherwise, holding three honour cards of three different colours in her hand in a last-ditch attempt, she gives calls in her fine voice, 'Two no-trumps!' Like the interest on debt, the rate of loss mounts apace. When the game is over, she signs in the accounts book bravely. By the end of the month, the poor husband signs on cheques mutely and I guess, remembers god in silence.

Most of the Indian officers, irrespective of race or religion, are members of the Chelmsford Club. Punjab, Sind, Gujarat, Maratha, Dravida, Utkala and Banga—no possible place of origin is unrepresented there. But the presence of the Punjabis is dominant; the Sikhs, in particular. They come in droves to play three sets of tennis in the afternoon and five rubbers of bridge in the evening. By the time they return home after three pegs of whiskey and a dinner of four courses, the calendar has already moved ahead a day. Their better halves follow them closely. A glance at a married Punjabi couple in a club easily conveys the meaning of the expression '*sahadharmini*' i.e. co-sharers on the path of dharma.

The club I was taken to by my friends is situated at the other end of the city. The subscription is paltry and members are not many. There are Bengalis, Madrassis, Assamese and a few from other provinces. This, too, is open to both sexes. Many of the ladies are Christians.

Whatever the register of the Club might indicate, female members seem to be in majority inside the club-room. Most of them were unmarried. Their complexions were dark, nails were red and cheeks, a dull grey. It only remains to be said that the last two were not natural, but courtesy foreign cosmetic companies. They wore rather strange clothes and their ornaments were even stranger.

One of the women was clad in what was practically a mosquito net with satin borders over a pink petticoat. In the case of another, the extremely economical use of thread in her lace blouse would redden one's ears if one were to raise one's eyes to look up at her.

Most were aged over thirty. Some personified the Euclidean straight line, some the ellipse in mathematics. In the geography of our womankind, temperate has no place—it's either North or South Pole. Some of them are teachers, some are nurses and some others are stenographers.

The Club has arrangements for badminton, carrom and table tennis. But, displaying style over play and false coyness over conversation, measure higher. A thirty-five year old bulky lady was trying to sell tickets of some benefit-drama. Her manner of speaking and conduct was provoking me time and again to intrude and say, 'Dear Lady, surely you believe that you are still on the right side of sixteen; but I feel obliged to remind you that it was over twenty years ago.'

I know that there's no point being angry with them. God denied them beauty and luck refused them riches. Their ancestry does not smack of aristocratic fame. Their age is on the rise, youth, almost past. The days of finding a match for them after elders compare horoscopes are nearly over. Their minds and bodies have grown tired, helping students to learn the gerundial infinitive by rote; annoyance has informed their chores. In passing thermometers and ice-bags to unknown, unrelated patients at whose bedside they keep night-vigil; despondency has crept into their life unawares, having typed 'with reference to your letter number...' endlessly in the office.

It's in the blood of a woman to build a home with near and dear ones. A small house, a devoted husband, one or two bonny babies —these are the elements of imagination which she has inherited over eons from her mother, grandmother and *ad seriatim*, from Eve, the earliest woman, the wife of Adam. This dream did not materialise in her life, the desire remained unsatisfied. She waited futilely so long, with a stricken heart and enflamed desire within. She might not have been a beauty, but she was healthy. But now her charm is lost, her natural tenderness is gone and modesty, her best ornament, is compromised. Eventually she strives to go conquer the unfathomable grief of her neglected heart,by occupying herself in one way or the other . Some are busying themselves in women's associations; some give talks on the radio; some, dolled up with rouge, powder and lipstick, flirt unabashedly with men.

Among the male members of the Club are college students, Secretariat employees, insurance agents, physicians and so forth. They are largely youths. Most of the married members are Christian, while the unmarried ones are Hindu. The reason is self-evident.

Education, civilisation and ideas from the West have brought in our country a new kind of environment. As a result, unthinkable change has occurred in our work and thought. Our food habits, the places we frequent, the clothes and accessories we use have all changed. Change has touched traditional ways, morals and objectives, thoughts and prejudices. We have, so long, regarded women only in relation to their male kinsmen. She might be our grandmother, aunt, sister, niece or sister-in-law. But that she might have a separate identity as a bosom-friend, besides being a mother, a wife, or a co-born, we have been made aware of, only recently.

As in the world of living beings, evolution is a phenomenon in the world of the psyche too. As a result, the relative values of diverse things, individuals and policies undergo a change over time, in our minds. The notion of the values of women in society too underwent changes from one era to another.

Once upon a time, society was matrifocal. From running the family to parental identity of a child and matters of succession, the entire gamut of societal construct used to be governed by the mother's directions, her definitions and relations. This matriarchal system became extinct gradually. The honour of the queen exceeded that of the king's mother. The family units of common people were also hit by this wave. Wives, not mothers, took to lording over families. Boys left the laps of their mothers and surrendered to being under the thumbs of their wives.

Of course, mothers were not happy at this change of hand. Some of them fought hard to retain their positions. It did not work. They lost summarily. All that they could gather for themselves was the eponymous notoriety in dramas and novels as thorny fault-pickers of daughters-in-law. The intelligent ones read the writing on the wall and accepted the inevitable. They did it without a word, but not with an ease of mind. The corpus of unvoiced complaints of all perturbed mothers of the world is full of angst against the modern homes lorded over by daughters-in-law. In European and American societies this lordship of wives is not questioned. After the marriage of a son, his mother is not a natural insider in his family. If she prefers to stay put, she would be there, not to call shots. Her presence is much like the silent 'h' in a word, it is there, but unuttered.

Even those days are no more when the term 'wife' was only construed as the ruler of household and as the begetter of progeny. A wife should have a friend in her, a secretary in her, an acolyte in her and even be accomplished in fine arts. But expecting so much from one person is appropriate only in poet Kalidas's epics, not in reality.

To the modern man, the call of the outer world is stronger. He attends office from ten to five, toils hard in mills and factories, moves around in the share market. He is then off to play tennis, or to bet on the race course or to join a meeting. Going to the club or the cinema is reserved for the night. In this arrangement, neither home nor wife has any real purpose. In olden times, the pursuit of religion required the participation of the wife; she played an important role in diverse religious and folk practices the year round. But now, even in India, religion seems to have no use but to secure votes at election time. Thus, in this day and age, romances are written, not about *sahadharmini*s but about *sahakarmini*s i.e. colleagues.

The functions of a wife and a home in a man's life are now minimal. To feed him there are restaurants, to comfort him there are boarding lodges, to care for him in distress are hospitals and nurses. The undeniable importance of a wife in rearing and educating children has been taken care of by boarding schools and children's homes. Accordingly, the sway of wives has now contracted to only camaraderie. She is more of a mate than a wife. She is neither the ruler nor the materfamilias, she is a friend.

For a woman too, a husband's role is less pervasive than before. Once upon a time, the need for a husband was mainly in maintaining, sustaining and protecting. But wives of today are not solely dependant on their husbands. If need be, they may even earn for themselves by toiling in an office.

So, the importance of a husband is no longer as the lord but only as a friend.

India could hardly fight shy of this neo-idealism. The wave has broken on her shores too. Our families are becoming smaller, ties with kith and kin are getting leaner. The village-centric base of our civilisation has been ruined, townships and colonies are expanding around mills and industries. Consequently, it is becoming inevitable that a new culture, a new outlook and perhaps a new religion of life will replace the old.

Nowadays, in this country, the confidante has appeared in the lives of men and women. Arguments may run on good and bad of it, articles may be featured in magazines citing references of sage Manu and sage Parashara, but its advent is unpreventable.

Our mentors were not entirely indifferent to the need of this intimacy in the life of men and women. But by deifying the husband as the ultimate preceptor and by reducing a wife to a nurse whose job is to wait upon him, the scope of being confidantes in conjugal life has been marred. In the fashion of a transferred epithet, these roles have been entrusted upon the sisters-in-law for a man and upon the brothers-in-law for a woman. I have no knowledge of any sweeter bond in our family circle.

Sita had found her confidant in Laxman and had no further need of a friend. Sage Valmiki, though advanced in years, was aware of this. Even though Panchali had no fewer than five husbands, her yearning for a brother-in-law was abiding. So, Veda Vyas, author of the *Mahabharata*, had to introduce on scene Lord Krishna. He became her confidant, one who gives protection in crises and remembered in times of joy.

The trappings of life these days are myriad and expensive. He who receives two hundred rupees a month can barely maintain his wife, let alone a sister-in-law! Girls are also aware that unless a dowry and a fund for gold ornaments are ready, many would not get a husband; a brother-in-law is far too much to expect! So the modern women have learnt the hard way that it's useless to expect too much and it's lucky to have one dependable and generous friend. Modern men have learnt through their wit that it is not worth being greedy; rather, it's desirable to have a single confidante, a soulmate.

In an ordinary orthodox Hindu family, a friendship between an unrelated man and woman is looked at askance. It's equally true of an ordinary Muslim family also. There isn't even any acknowledgement of a female friend. Indeed, the first unrelated woman a man comes close to is his wife. Thus the 'England-returned' gather in parties and at the clubs, youths flock together in the large well-appointed drawing rooms of senior corporate and government bosses. They address some as Lolita-*di*, some as Veena-*bhabhi*, while others have Ms or Mrs prefixed before their names—Ms Gupta, Ms Ayengar or Mrs Sonera Zaheer.

Nine

She, who arranged the moonlight picnic at Firoz Shah Kotla on the evening of thirtieth March has gathered fame in New Delhi society as an ideal hostess. She is pretty, witty and her conversation is melodious. She has that rare ability to both give and partake of pleasure liberally in an assembly of friends.

Firoz Shah Kotla is the remnant of the fifth avatar of Delhi as a capital city. During the reign of Prithviraj, the last Hindu emperor of India, the township of Delhi was at Mehrauli, close to present-day Qutub Minar. Sometime back, the Archaeology Department has partly excavated the oldest capital town's wall from under the earth. According to a legend, Prithviraj had erected the Qutub Minar to fulfil his beloved daughter's desire of enjoying a scenic view of the river Yamuna.Every afternoon, after completeing her grooming, the princess climbed to the top and saw the waters of the Yamuna in the distance. Historians, however, do not believe this story. Their opinion is that Emperor Qutubuddin Aibak had commenced building this highest victory tower in the world and Altamash finished its construction.

The second city of Delhi was established by Sultan Ala-ud-din Khilji. During his reign, fierce Mughal robbers invaded India and reached Delhi after razing many towns and villages to the ground, killing and looting innumerable people. It was not easy to resist them in the plains of Delhi. The Sultan retreated to Qutub. The Mughals occupied, per force, the adjacent area of Delhi, looted the riches and wealth of the amirs and the omrahas and inflicted ruin over the ploughed land of ordinary farmers. Rendered sick and tired by the ferocity of the unbearable heat of the Delhi summer, the band of rogue invaders left Delhi eventually. With a view to protecting the city from such onslaughts in the future, Ala-ud-din erected a new township, named Siri and fortified it with a protective wall. In the town the sultan had built for himself a very expensive palace which had one thousand pillars. Today, there is not even a trace left of that palace.

Ala-ud-din Khilji was a warrior of rare courage. He had, in his blood, the fervent desire to expand his kingdom through war expeditions. He defeated the Rajputs and annexed Chittor. He was the first to establish Islamic rule in the Deccan. To perpetuate his victories, he initiated the erection of a second Qutub, right beside the first Qutub. It would be twice the size of the first Qutub, this what he had in mind. But his lifespan was too short to see through to the end of the work. The remnants of this new-fangled, half-finished Qutub makes the visitors curious to date. Memorials to Siri are preserved only in the research of archeologists and to an extent, in the ruins of the wall at Biratnagar.

Firozabad was established by Sultan Firoz Shah Tughluq. Naming the capital after the monarch is nothing new in the annals of Islamic rule. Firoz Shah Tughluq was the best among the Muslim monarchs of the fourteenth century. For thirty-seven long years at a stretch, he wielded the royal sceptre with great valour. Of all the Islamic rulers of Delhi—with only the exception of Aurangzeb—he was the most advanced in age. He was above sixty when he ascended the throne after the death of Muhammad bin Tughluq.

The name of Muhammad bin Tughluq is notorious in history as a fickle-minded and imprudent monarch. But notwithstanding that, there is hardly any scope to disagree that he also had many good qualities becoming of a king. He was a polyglot, a poet, a mathematician and an ace scribe. He had renown also as a brave warrior and as a generous donor. In contrast though, there was no dearth of condemnation for his cruelty. In the autobiography of Ibn Batuta, the famous Arabian traveller, is found a brief but exact description of Muhammad bin Tughluq,

> 'King Muhammad simply has no match in terms of charity and slaughtering. Along the road he takes to tread, he makes one or the other dirt poor man rich and one or the other living man dead. Hundreds of episodes of his generosity and cruelty co-exist and do the rounds very briskly among people.'

Ibn Batuta himself served as the Qazi or the chief judge of Delhi under him.

Muhammad had many inventive ideas but he lacked everyday common sense. He had a penchant for conducting experiments in diverse subjects. Most of these experiments met with fatal ends. The transfer of the capital from North India to the Deccan a number of times, the mass exodus of residents of Delhi to Daulatabad and return thereafter, the introduction of copper currency to replace silver, Chinese expeditions—these are some instances of his ruinous enterprises that we've read about in school history books during our childhood.

Towards the end of his days, Muhammad had laid siege with his battalion outside the fortress in Thatta, near present-day Karachi. One morning a fisherman there, netted a strange fish from the river Indus. It was brought before the king. Muhammad was suddenly seized with the idea of testing the palatability of that completely unknown fish. He ignored the requests and advice of all present and tasted that fish. It was his last experiment on earth. He breathed his last that very day.

Muhammad had genius as well as physical strength. At that time, in the stretch between Siri, the capital of Ala-ud-din Khilji and ancient Mehrauli, many palatial buildings and pleasure gardens of the wealthy people of Delhi had come up gradually. But owing to the absence of adequate protective measures, these had been exposed to attacks by Mughal robbers. Muhammad built his own palace there. He surrounded the stretch between Siri to Mehrauli by an impenetrable wall. The new township was named 'Jahanpanah'–refuge of the world. In the land adjacent to the palace, he dug a large lake to provide potable water. In the village of Khidki, a little way off from the Qutub, one can see, even today, the remains of the wall. On its surface is evident the sign of the water inlet into the lake he dug.

The excavation work in a site close to the present-day Qutub Road, by the Government's Archeological Department, has unearthed Muhammad's great bath, his zenana and his famous rampart, sitting in which he watched the parade of his army daily. Muhammad had also constructed a large apartment after the style of Ala-ud-din's one-thousand pillar apartment, remnants of which still amaze curious visitors.

Firoz Shah Tughluq became the monarch after Muhammad's death. He was Muhammad's kinsman and the commander of his army. He returned to Delhi from Sind with his arms and men and readily took over the kingdom. It may not be known to many that Firoz Shah happened to be the first monarch in India who had both Hindu and Muslim blood in his veins. His mother was a Rajput woman.

The combined influence of the two different religions had lent a certain uniqueness to his character. He was renowned as a learned and religious man and he displayed genuine concern for the welfare of his subjects. The first artificial irrigation system of the Islamic era was implemented by him. The canal which is now known as the Western Yamuna Canal was dug by him. Arising from the main stream of the Yamuna at Karnal, a branch of the canal has entered Delhi while another has flown to Hissar. During Firoz Shah's time the canal was much wider. By a royal decree of Emperor Shah Jahan, Ali Mardan Khan, the then chief of Public Works, dredged and cleaned the canal. It wouldn't be too out of context to mention that Emperor Shah Jahan, too, had Hindu influence in his blood. His mother also hailed from Rajputana. This canal was laid waste for the second time when Ahmad Shah Abdali led a siege of Delhi and later, through the efforts of the English rulers, the canal was restored.

Firoz Shah had a passion for erecting edifices. This, too, was similar to Emperor Shah Jahan's inclinations. The two upper stories of the Qutub in white marble is Firoz Shah's feat. It was he who restored the earthquake-hit part of the Qutub. There, in the ridge, adjacent to the Hindu Rao Hospital, still exists the ruin of the hunter's house erected by him.

Although there existed no less than three townships at Siri, Vijaymandal and Qutub, Firoz Shah founded another new township by the river Yamuna. Right on the bank of the Yamuna, he built his palace Firoz Shah Kotla. Today, entering through its wide doorway, a large grass-covered courtyard comes into view on the left. Once upon a time the royal court of Firoz Shah was held there. Our picnic party gathered at that very spot today.

It's not that small a party—about twelve in all, men and women together. But the hostess has arranged adequate provisions for double that number to enjoy an expansive meal at ease.

The man most worthy of drawing attention in the picnic party was Mr Khosla. He is widely known, especially among women. Women are organising an exhibition; who is the one volunteering at the gate? Mr Khosla. The Women's Association is raising funds for the benefit of people affected by the Damodar floods. Who is accompanying the girls from door to door? Mr Khosla. Buying wool from Chandni Chowk for Mrs Mukherjee, taking rounds in shops in search of Ponds cold cream for Mrs Swaminathan; for all these, there's Mr Khosla. That there might be a gathering of women, whether in a party, picnic, association or assembly in New Delhi, yet Mr Khosla is absent, is unimaginable.

He is robust, albeit shorter than ordinary Punjabis. He brushes his hair to the back. His long sideburns extend up to the middle of his cheeks, mimicking the silent-era film-star Douglas Fairbanks. His moustache is styled on Hitler's. He wears brown corduroy trousers, tapering at the heels. There's a hip pocket at the seat. Tucked inside it is a monogrammed long silver cigarette case, within the womb of which is room for fifty cigarettes. A knee-length gabardine coat, the lower pockets of which are cut in the shape of a crescent moon, over a silk shirt. A crimson tie printed with blue creepers and herbs. A green felt hat worn slightly low. Either combination-shoes or buckled suede-shoes adorn his feet. A pair of sunglasses with a thick shell frame covers his eyes in the daytime, whether sunny or not. Like a wristwatch on a lady's hand, Mr Khosla's goggles are decorative rather than utilitarian.

Dissenting views exist on Mr Khosla's profession. Some say he is a contractor, some say he acts as an agent of two or three insurance companies and what still others say could be translated as following; he's nothing but a loafer. On his visiting card, he uses the term 'Merchant' to describe himself, a generic word added after his name that might describe anybody from the titan of an industry to a rustic cut-piece seller in a non-descript marketplace somewhere. But whatever might his calling be, he is always busy. Even in these days of petrol rationing, he is to be seen at all hours speeding across the city in his Baby Austin. If he stumbles upon anybody known, he spares a minute and hastily adds, 'Well then, my brother, I'm very busy at the moment. I'll see you again soon.'

With great enthusiasm Mr Khosla served various delicacies to the assembled ladies. While rushing here and there, a plate of sandwiches in hand, he barely averted a fall. He busied himself with a tray of *sandesh*; with liberal use of 'please' and 'for-my-sake', he coaxed the belles to have two extra pieces of pastry. A young lady was asking for a glass of water from someone. Mr Khosla happened to be passing by. The moment the request reached his ears, he bolted and charged around saying, 'Water, please, some water, water for Ms Upadhyay,' so very anxiously that it appeared, unless he found water handy, he might readily dash to Mount Kailash like the mythical Bhagirath to get the Ganges flowing.

Mrs Subba Rao proposed that we take a look around the place. All that was there to see was a mosque built by Firoz Shah. The Sultan used to visit the mosque with his retinue to offer prayers on *jumma* day. It is not exaggeration to imagine that this mosque commanded exceptional importance in that time. Its ruinous condition today, of course, does not convey its lost grace. But its structural orderliness is worthy of attention. In English we call it 'proportion'. Proportion is the hallmark of the mosque at Firoz Shah Kotla as well as the other palatial ruins here.

The synthesis of the Hindu and Islamic styles in Indian architecture found a new expression during Firoz Shah's era. The North Indian style of Hindu architecture was completely different in the pre-Islamic era. It is still evident in very old Hindu temples. Now known as the Jain style, its best instance is possibly the famous temple atop Mount Abu in Rajputana.

In the Hindu architecture of that era, there was no use of semi-circular arches. Its unique feature was quadrangular pillars. The pillars were carved with designs. Some were of Hindu gods, some were of floral arrangements, while others were of bells and trees. An evidence of the carving skills and inventiveness of the architects of yore are found in the design and ornamentation of the stone pillars. There was no use of domes either. Parallel arrangement of slabs of stones, one on another, over the quadrangular pillars, used to be brought in the middle, by drawing them close together from two ends. This structure, instead of arches, on the upper part of gates, windows and entrances, looks a lot like the stratified steps of a staircase. An arch is more capable of supporting weight and was in vogue in Europe and in Central Asia.

A change in this style first occurred at the end of the twelfth century. Qutubuddin Aibak of the Slave Dynasty wanted to first erect a mosque upon his arrival in Delhi, wherein he might sit down to send his daily prayers to Allah, beseeching more wealth, more power and most of all, profound peace. Naturally, he sought to build a prayer house in the style with which he was familiar from his childhood days in his native country, Afghanistan. The mosques there had pointed arches, built upon vaults shaped like the curly braces used in mathematics.

The Romans used circular arches; the Arabs preferred to use pointed arches. Pundits have concluded that the first architectural instance of pointed arches is the mosque at Samara in central Iraq, built in the sixth century AD. The Hindu masons were not aware of its construction technique. It was not feasible to bring Muslim masons from Kabul or Qandahar. As a consequence, the architectural style preserved in the first mosque in Delhi was not a synthesis of Hindu and Islamic styles but a fusion of the two. The proof is evident in the mosque adjacent to the Qutub. The semi-circular pattern in the portico and the entrance to that mosque are not built upon actual arches. There is no key-stone.

The tradition of carving deities, flowers and creepers were not a tradition in Islamic architecture. Quotes from the Koran used to be inscribed on walls and arches.

The Indian masons who worked to construct the mosque of Qutubuddin Aibak possessed little knowledge of the Arabic script and the Koranic text. So they painted trees over the artificial arch and somehow made an effort to inscribe Arabic words on it. The sign of Hindu architecture is more apparent on the plinth from which the mosque rises. Its pillars were certainly taken from some Hindu temple. Islamic rulers at that time had no qualms about looting and plundering. In fact, by making open use of the pilferage, they built victory monuments for posterity to appreciate their misdeeds.

Inspired to expand the mosque built by Aibak, Sultan Altamash brought Muslim architects and masons from Ghazni. They introduced in India the geometrical methods of Islamic illustrations. In the era of the Khilji dynasty, many more Muslim masons arrived from Afghanistan. They pioneered the use of actual arches with key-stones in place of quadrangular pillars, domes in place of pyramidal roofs commonly called '*shikhara*' and embellishment with geometric lines instead of bells, flowers and trees. Islamic architecture was then fully established in India. Allai-darwaza, adjacent to Qutub and Jamatkhana mosque of Nizamuddin are instances of pure Islamic architecture of that era.

During Tughluq dynastic rule, particularly at the time of Firoz Shah, Hindu architectural methods were found to have reappeared in palaces, forts and other buildings. The innate nature of prevalent architecture of the period was without grandeur and adornments. Those edifices were made of ordinary stones layered over with lime and brick-dust; there was not much use of white and red stones, typically popular during Khilji dynasty and later, during the Mughal reign. Adopting preventive measures against the attacks of Mughal robbers and the Deccan expedition had probably strained the royal purse before time, for Firoz Shah to spend lavishly on expensive stones in construction. Neither was it unlikely that owing to the frequent change of abode of the residents of Delhi due to Muhammad bin Tughluq's diktat, a paucity of skilled stone-masons had come about.

The most remarkable features of the edifices built by Firoz Shah included the use of quadrangular pillars, the use of Hindu methods of construction rather than arches in doorways and porches and decoration of walls with blooming lotuses. Ideal example of this is found in the later part of Hauz Khas, built by Firoz Shah.

The passage to ascend to the building, at Firoz Shah Kotla over which stands the Ashokan Pillar, beside the mosque, is not very difficult. Steps are a bit steep indeed. But so long as our companion, saviour of damsels-in-distress, Mr Khosla is there, the girls needn't worry. Standing at the bottom, he watched over till all the ladies ascended the steps to the building. He lent a helping hand to the more familiar and extended his hand, saying, 'May I?' to the recent acquaintance.

It is said that the part of the palace where the Ashokan Pillar was mounted, fell inside Firoz Shah's household. The pillar is made of stone. This pillar was erected in a village near Ambala by Emperor Ashoka, nearly two-hundred and fifty years before the birth of Christ. Firoz Shah caught a glimpse of the pillar, once when he was returning from a pleasure-hunting trip. He had profound interest in and passion for ancient works of art. He arranged the pillar to be lifted from there to his capital town at Firoz Shah Kotla.

Hundreds of labourers pulled the pillar on a forty-two wheel cart. On top of the pillar was a golden umbrella. At a later period, Jat invaders to Delhi looted it. After many years, the Pali inscriptions on the pillar have been finally deciphered. The pillar displays one of the hundreds of edicts which Emperor Ashoka propagated all over India as a disciple of Lord Buddha, beseeching men and women to practice non-violence and benevolence to all living beings.

Standing by the Ashokan Pillar, the flowing water of the river Yamuna can be seen at a short distance. It's not far-fetched to make out that in Firoz Shah's time the stream of the Yamuna would touch the feet of Firoz Shah Kotla.

After the descent, we all sat in a circle in the open field. To one side of us was a small pool of water. Locals call it *baoli*. In fierce summer days, the Sultan used to bathe in this pool and take rest on the stone dais on its bank.

Someone said, 'If we're carrying playing cards, a round can be played.'

Our skipper readily took out from her case two decks of pristine cards, printed pads and pencils.

All joined in an ovation, 'Indeed, this is farsightedness! One who can anticipate the needs of all hours is the god in waiting.'

Dr Adhikary, a lieutenant in the army, is the oldest among us and is of a very jocular nature with a good sense of humour. He wears his shock of white hair as a cover-up for his inherent youthful disposition. He has come from the cantonment ten kilometres away to join the picnic. He is an ace contract bridge player. He rejoiced, 'Cripps' dialogue is ongoing now. If there is Swaraj, we'll make her the president. The first woman President in independent India is Mrs Bijaya Banerjee. Let's cheer in the name of Bijaya Banerjee.'

All yelled in a chorus, 'Jai ho!'

I objected, 'Colonel, the word "President" reminds us of a picture of a grey-haired old woman who is past her prime. Rather, let us call her a queen.'

The Colonel agreed readily, 'Right you are! Queen suits her better: the second lady empress of Delhi. Sultana Bijaya follows Sultana Razia. Jai ho Maharani Bijaya! Vande Mataram, Allah-ho-Akbar, Hip-hip-hooray!'

The Sultana-in-waiting asked smilingly, 'Do you say all three in one breath?'

'Certainly, I do. I'm to keep Gandhi-Maharaj, Janab Jinnah and the British Government happy. Whoever has the power, I'm with him. The faster one changes one's views in keeping with the situation—they are called progressives in English!'

Mr Jubeiry has just become an ICS. He studied for some time in the London School of Economics. He still retains a devotion to socialism. He said, 'Queen smacks of monarchism. In this era of democracy it won't do...'

Colonel replied, 'It'll certainly do! Monarchism is the way of life in every household and a government outside home can't be run by it? My dear, you are still young, much is left there to learn. The item named democracy is found only in the book by Harold Lasky. Ask Mr Banerjee, if the window-curtains in his house would be green or blue, if bitter gourd gravy curry or diced vegetables tossed and steamed in a drop of oil would be served at lunch, were these at his discretion or were they run by the writ of command of the queen? Once you marry, you come to know that in Her Majesty's government there is everything but the Leader of the Opposition.'

A huge roar of laughter ensued.

The fair lady blushed with modesty and self-satisfaction. To contain the issue she looked at me and said, 'No more conversation please. Let's start the game.'

With clasped hands I said, 'Forgive me, but I am a complete greenhorn in this.'

'What? How unusual! Well then, let's forget the game. You sing us a song.'

'Woe me! Better you ask me to jump from the top of the Qutub. Come what may, I can give it a try for your sake. But if I start crooning, the desire to jump will be reversed on you.'

Mr Banerjee said, 'Then you recite us a poem, Tagore's poem.'

I replied, 'Between cramming inflected word-forms to pass in Sanskrit examinations during boyhood and later, memorising sections of the jurisprudence for a pass in law, when did I find time to memorise a poem?'

Mrs Banerjee said, 'Well, then, tell us a story.'

Dr Adhikary amended the proposal, 'It should be a love story.'

I replied with a grin, 'Colonel, if it's a matter of love then it must be a story for sure, not fact. But even such a story is not known to me. I may tell you a ghost story if you like. Do you know that here, beside this *baoli,* on your right where Mrs Mitra sits, there is the stain of royal blood? Emperor Alamgir the second was slaughtered here.'

'Oh my God!' exclaimed Mrs Mitra. She sprang to her feet and resettled herself in the middle of the group. Ever so often, she apprehensively looked at the ends of her sari as if a few drops of blood had actually spoilt it. Everyone enjoyed a bout of laughter. But, it was not that other women present were not even a bit perturbed.

Mr Khosla became extremely worried for Mrs Mitra. He kept repeating that the ladies should not have been frightened in this manner. Had somebody suffered a shock out of fright then things could take a dangerous turn, etc. and so forth?

The leader was not to be contained. She insisted, 'Well, tell us your ghost story. It should be real ghost stuff. Not fiction.'

'Mrs Banerjee, ghosts are always fictitious. Ghost stories are even more so. But, I regret, I don't even know that.'

The lady swung her head briskly, 'No, no, this won't do. You are only giving us the slip. No card game, no singing, not even storytelling. Please perform something.'

The Colonel remarked, 'Tut-tut, you are spoiling your case. If you really can't perform anything, you won't get a berth in our Queen's government.'

The lady said, 'Exactly so. What do I do with you? You can't be a court musician as you can't sing. I can't engage you as a court-pundit as you can't recite poems. You can't tell stories that I'll make a friend out of you! What an arch-idler you are, what would you be?'

With clasped palms I said, 'I shall tend the flowers in your ladyship's garden.'

A huge sway of laughter ensued.

Ten

At present we share the same professional detachment to the fate of the Cripps Mission as that of a physician who writes prescriptions for a patient who he knows is destined to die soon and has no chance to recover. The assembled journalists at New Delhi have no misgivings about its failure. Now the question does not involve an unanticipated recovery at the fag-end; the question is when the Mission's failure will be officially announced.

Curiously, even a couple of weeks before, there were no reasons of apprehending this outcome for emissary Cripps. On the contrary, most people had hoped for the establishment of a national government in India as the result of an honourable settlement between Britain and India through this political discourse.

In December 1941, Japan announced war on Britain and America. On the very first day, Pearl Harbour was ravaged. Only after three days, the *Prince of Wales* and the *Repulse*, the pride and vanguard of the British Navy, sank in the Pacific after being bombed. In no time, the Japanese snatched away Malay and Hong Kong. On 16 February 1942, Singapore, the best-fortified British base in the Far East—commonly perceived by all as impenetrable —fell.

In its annals of two-hundred years of British rule, for the first time India faced an enemy on land and water. The anxiety of authority figures, panic among commoners and the loose tongues of gullible ignorants gave rise to a variety of rumours tinged with terror.

Faced with such a situation, Prime Minister Churchill announced in the House of Commons that the War Cabinet had reached consensus on a 'just and final solution' to the present and future problems of India and the Lord Privy Seal, Sir Stafford Cripps himself, would be proceeding to India to secure the agreement of Indian leaders on the War Cabinet's proposal.

Ever since the beginning of the Second World War, the demands for a nationalist India by the Indians have been ignored time and again. The Congress's proposal of cooperation has been rejected over and over again. A few months ago, Marshal Chiang Kai-shek and Madame came to visit India. Through an open statement, they requested Britain to most expeditiously transfer the real political power to Indians. Soon after, President Roosevelt objected, in no uncertain terms, to Churchill's comments, pointing out that the Atlantic Charter is for the entire world; no nation ought to be deprived of its benefit. And almost concurrently, Mr Evatt, the Foreign Minister of Australia, conceded in the Australian Parliament the demand for independence of India as just and proper and said that the Australians were sympathetic to that demand.

The conservative authority in Britain, no doubt, was very distraught with the increasing outpouring of support from the nations of the world in favour of India's struggle for self-rule. But even more significant was the reason implicit in the Prime Minister's announcement; not that it was born of any generosity, request, solicitation, or advice. The reason was the consequence of real, hard events. On the eighth of March, British imperialism ended in Burma with the fall of Rangoon. The necessity of appeasing the agitated Indian public and swing its opinion in favour of the British was never felt so essential before. On the eleventh of March, Churchill announced the Cripps Mission.

It must be admitted that the Prime Minister's announcement aroused unprecedented enthusiasm in India. The newspapers and the public here heartily welcomed this new enterprise of the British War Cabinet. Perhaps finally Britain was keen to actually solve the Indian problem; had agreed to transfer power.

The reason behind this favourable attitude in India was the faith reposed by Indians on the person who was authorised by the War Cabinet to hold dialogues. India regards Sir Stafford Cripps as one of the few indophile Englishmen of this century. Cripps had visited India twice before. He is directly acquainted with the ways and policies of the Congress. He is a dear friend of Pandit Jawaharlal Nehru. He wielded his pen more than once, wishing for an early end to British rule in India. Not long ago, only after seven weeks of proclamation of war in Europe, Cripps had remarked with deep conviction in the House of Commons, 'The just and rightful demand for independence by Indians is still unfulfilled owing to the obstinacy of the British Government, not because of the Congress's rigidity. Communal discord is only a pretext'.

The efforts of this very man at reaching an amicable settlement is about to be aborted. The difference of opinion at present is centred around the question of defence. According to the proposal of the British Government, the defence of the country will lie solely in the hands of a commander-in-chief. The Congress demand is that the defence of the country should be the responsibility of its people. Inspiration and encouragement are required to be instilled into the minds of the people of the country to bear that responsibility and this would be possible only by an Indian defence secretary and not by a foreign commander-in-chief.

Congress was in agreement with the proposal of devolving the direct responsibility of conducting war on a commander-in-chief. The Congress didn't disagree about conferring maximum autonomy for that end. But, unless the principal responsibility of protecting our country lies with an Indian defence secretary, there will be no meaning in achieving self-determination. Particularly while at war, other problems and logistics of a country are largely influenced by the bigger issue of protecting the country. The actual measure of achieving independence and responsibility is determined by the absolute right to the defence of the country.

To deny the substance of this argument was beyond Cripps. So he forwarded an alternative. The commander-in-chief will discharge the responsibilities of conducting war as the war secretary, while another elected member will be associated with the protection of the country as the defence secretary.

Good idea! But then, what about their line of work? Cripps produced a list of suggested duties of the proposed new defence secretary. The list included the following: (1) supply of petrol; (2) stationery, i.e. purchase and maintainence of stock—paper, pencil, nib, ink, pens—and printing of various forms; (3) running the Canteen, etc..

It is difficult to read through the list with a straight face. There are several age-old tricks that women would play on newly married sons-in-law—putting bits of chillies inside a betel-leaf and offering the *paan* to him, coiling a piece of cloth inside a puffed *luchi* or adding salt instead of sugar in sherbet. But when the issue of the hour is the discussion between the leaderships of two countries, staking the fate of four hundred million people, certainly such a mean joke like putting marbles under a chair to disrupt one's movements and cause one to tumble down is not expected!

That afternoon, I was invited by a reporter friend to a tea party at the Imperial Hotel. My friend is not a supporter of the Congress; in his opinion, Gandhiji is an unpractical idealist given to dreaming, lacking in worldly wisdom. He is neither an Indian, nor an American—he is an Englishman. He said, with much annoyance, 'Which enemy of Britain prepared the list and passed it over to Cripps? Could it be a fifth columnist hired by the Japanese?'

Not impossible.

My friend was genuinely enraged. He said, 'Petrol, stationery, canteen! Why not toothpicks and broomsticks?'

For the last one week we've been discussing, in ever so many nuances of expression, that Pt Jawaharlal Nehru would be the first defence secretary of India! Let us just imagine once, Pt Nehru is broadcasting an appeal in his inimitable language, to inspire the nation to resist the Japanese invasion and with it, is reading out his list of jobs, 'petrol, pencils, nibs, pins...'. Apparently there is a limit to all things in the world. Does 'all' exclude inanity? Or derision?

The British authority has to say this: the responsibility of protecting the country during the war is Britain's. That responsibility is not confined only to the uncountable millions of India, but extends to the group of Allied nations with whom Britain is fighting, united against the Axis powers. That responsibility they couldn't shirk.

Protecting the territory of India is complex for a number of reasons. There is no equivalent of a 'National Army' in India. The army in India has been formed with professional sepoys. During the reign of the East India Company, sepoys used to be recruited from different parts of the country. One by one, the Company occupied towns, provinces and states and gradually added to the force of the sepoys, tempting them with the offer of a salaried income.

Soon after the Sepoy Mutiny, Queen Victoria took over from the Company. The army also came under the control of the queen. Things started to change. The English authority felt the need to adopt extreme caution against the native sepoys as a consequence of the Sepoy Mutiny. A British division was attached to every two Indian divisions, so that in the event of any sign of hostility on the part of the Indians, matters could be contained forthwith. Prior to the Mutiny, there used to be one British Division attached to every six Indian Divisions. Not a single Indian was recruited in the Artillery Division till 1935. Before this war, the number of officers of Indian origin in the army were only a handful and those few were never promoted above the rank of a Major. By military standards, it appears that the Indians were still to achieve 'majority'!

The most stringent precautionary arrangement was applied in the selection of men for the army. By the artificial division of the people of the country as belonging to the martial or non-martial races, almost everybody, except residents of Punjab and the Frontier Provinces, have been carefully kept out of the Indian Army. Nonetheless, anyone who has had a little brush with history knows it well that the English gained control of the major part of this land only by dint of the military skills of the sepoys and sentries of Bengal and Madras who have now been repudiated as 'non-martial'. Those English politicians, who for easily understandable reasons, are ecstatic with deferential praise over the military skills of the Muslims and are prone to shed tears for the imagined helplessness of the Hindus in the event of a civil strife in the absence of the English, that gamut of indophiles may be reminded that during the phase of expansion of the British power in India, the people from whom they received maximum resistance were the Sikhs and the Marathas, recognised as the best military powers then. Of these two, the religion of the first was pure Hinduism and of the second was a variant of the reformed Hinduism. Neither was Islam.

What might be the reason for this preferential attitude towards the Punjab and Frontier Provinces by the military administration? Some opine that people from the North are usually taller and stronger than those from the Southern or the Eastern parts of India. But this reason alone does not suffice as the sole factor in determining militarily inclined clans. Then the Gorkhas would not have worn khaki ever. Particularly when the practice of gauging martial skills of soldiers that were reliant only on physical prowess has come to an end with the invention of fire arms.

The advantage of securing men for the army from particular regions is that it creates a new caste system. Serving in the army becomes, in many cases, hereditary. By lineal succession from grandfather to father to son, the vocation extends through the bloodline and by serving the same army through generations, a firm commitment develops. People develop the feeling that they are an integral part of that army. This is on the same lines as the hiring of a cashier, a head clerk or a broker of the large European companies in Calcutta. For a foreign ruler, the empathy that is evoked towards the instrument of rule in the minds of the ruled is of no little significance as a secret of success.

There is an even more important reason of course. That is political. One cannot but accept that even some time ago the North-Western part of India was devoid of political awareness. Punjab was the only province where the natives did not resort to armed struggle against the British during the Sepoy Mutiny. In recent times also, the sign of national awakening is feebler in Punjab than in other provinces of India. Those who compose panegyrics on the patriotism of Punjab, citing examples of the Gadar Party and the Komagatamaru, might do well to remember that those Punjabis were inspired to patriotic fervour abroad, not in their own land. The ordinary Punjabis are happy with living out a great lifestyle, earning a fat salary, enjoying a variety of food and expensive clothes; they don't spend much thought over the country. The likes of Bhagat Singh are only exceptions, not a rule.

The Bengalis are most unwanted in the Indian army. The *Manusamhita* of the army places them in the outcast category. No surprises there. Since the beginning of the twentieth century, they have been protesting and incessantly fighting against British rule in India with immense spirit. The awakening of modern nationalism in India occurred here. In the nationalist struggle, mothers have let go of their sons, girls have lent inspiration, boys have laid down their lives. To abate their influence, Curzon had partitioned Bengal, Hardinge shifted the capital and McDonald instituted the Communal Award. Oh damn! Wouldn't allowing them in the army ruin us all? It would be pertinent to mention here that the first portent of Sepoy Mutiny had showed up here, in an army barrack at Barrackpore.

This partiality in the name of 'military type' has undoubtedly benefited the British rulers. It's true that the British rulers have taken good care of the worldly well-being of this 'military type' for fear of slackening of loyalty owing to any wants or complaints. To an ordinary poor villager, the pay and pension in the military is lucrative. Besides that, many have received *jagir*s (fiefdoms) after superannuation.

Punjab supplies soldiers and horses for the army and so has enjoyed better affection and attention of the authorities. Agricultural development and healthcare is more advanced in that region. Cooperative movement and agricultural research have started there; the most amazing and expensive artificial irrigation system of the British era in India can be found in the Punjab and Sind provinces. Most of the farmers there possess lands full of standing crops, cowsheds full of cows and an array of army medals to display in the showcase. There they reverentially address the sahibs as '*Huzur*' (Master), the police officers as 'Me Lord' and the government as 'Sarkar Bahadur'. Who might pay heed to Swaraj there?

But, for how long can a surge of floodwater remain amenable to control by sand blocks? What worry would there have been if the sea abided by the orders of King Canute? Despite all deterrents and precautions, the march of patriotism has spread far and wide, by and by. East, west, north and south—no corner of India is now beyond its reach. Khan Abdul Gaffur Khan is the stalwart of this in the Western Frontier.

It's no longer that safe to train these simple and devoid-of-all-connection-with-politics people of this much-favoured region against the interests of their own country and its people. Perhaps many do not know the fact that during the passive resistance movement of 1930, a batch of Hindu Garhwal soldiers relinquished arms, defying the order to fire at Muslim volunteers at Peshawar. The news was banned and the press didn't publish it here.

The communal make-up of the army until 1941 was 35 per cent Muslim, 23 per cent Sikh and 42 per cent Hindu. What is to note here is that, the much touted calumny against the Hindus of their martial incapacity is not supported even by these statistics!

The military policy of India saw change for the first time, although only a little, after the First World War ended. A decision was taken to Indianise a small fraction of the armed forces that had so far been exclusively commanded over by the European officers. Indians came to be regarded as fit for receiving King's commission in the Army and an Indian Sandhurst was established at Dehradun to impart training to the Indian commanders and officers.

In the course of the current war this Indianisation has moved apace. Of course, it is not driven by any soft spot for the Indians. It's Britain's own necessity. Those Indians, who did not even have any chance of entry into the army previously being classified as a 'non-military type' might now be an officer in the Army. The removal of this hurdle though, I believe, has not helped the Bengalis even now to substantially increase their presence in the Army, although their number in the Airforce is not that dismal. A few of them have already earned acclaim as ace pilots.

So far, the bases for the territorial protection of India were located in the north-west. All the cannons of the commander-in-chief were aimed at the Afridis. Like a one-eyed deer, the military commanders realised after the bombing of Pearl Harbour that danger knocks at the most unsuspected corner of the country.

Going by the principle of warfare, the first line of defence for India against Japan should be the Navy. It's not in place. The water- and sea-ways are under enemy control. The professional army of British and Indian origin are not adequately equipped with modern weaponry here and moreover, their bases are located far away from the probable theatres of war, at the other end of the country.

Whether the question as to what would constitute the ways and means of self-defence in the case of India against this impending danger has actually arisen in the mind of the military authority can't be known. But common people who have neither arms nor any war experience have raised this question in their mind. At last, a man directed an answer to this question. His name is Pt Jawaharlal Nehru.

Jawaharlal came up with a plan to raise an army of five million Indian men. Nehru is the descendant of a Pandit from Kashmir. Rajkaul, superior ancestor, was a renowned scholar well-versed in Parsi and Sanskrit texts and Laxmi Narayan Nehru, his great-grandfather, was a famous pleader in the Mughal courts. The son of an advocate, Jawaharlal himself had embarked on his career as a lawyer. Regarding the defence of the country, first of all, it was he who planned mass martial training. He who thinks of and for the people, we call him '*janagana-mana-adhinayaka*' (the leader in the minds of the people).

Weaponry? We are certainly in need of it. To provide weapons to the five million soldiers, new mills and workshops have to be established and the existing ones are required to be expanded. But it will take time. The enemy won't wait that long to strike. Panditji had the opportunity of studying deeply, from close quarters, the wartime organisations and military strategies of people's militias in Spain and China. The army in Spain was formed by members drawn from societies of cultivators and labourers. A number of army commanders grew out of those who had ploughed land or woven cloth in their early life. Jawaharlal planned to bring in trainers of defence techniques from China.

The maximum advantage of such a force is its mobility. Hand bombs make up for a lack of rifles.

The villagers were anxious to help this militia everywhere. Food to abate their appetites and shelter to save people from danger were provided by them. Inspired by patriotic fervour for the country, this battalion was unique. They were not like salaried soldiers under European command who mechanically carried out the orders of superiors.

According to hearsay, some of the British generals were of the opinion to try out this plan with due regards and it was also heard that Major Tom Wintringham would come to India from England to take up the charge of training this army. Wintringham was associated with the army of the Republican Party at the time of war against Franco in Spain. But whoever had hoped that the British Government would favourably consider Pt Nehru's plan is lacking in experience on the human character. He should have known that British proposals do not speak of soldiers and weaponry; it speaks of petrol, stationery and the canteen. Rule Britannia, Britannia rules the slaves!

I was returning to my place from the Imperial Hotel. As I stepped out of the gate, suddenly a car pulled its brakes and screeched to a halt just ahead. The passenger craned his neck and said, 'Hey, you're our Bonchka, indeed! What on earth are you doing here? Come on in.'

Bonchka is neither the name my parents christened me with at birth, nor something relatives call me by. It was a nickname invented by my pre-teen classmates in school to vex me. After a disagreement over the right of ownership on a wooden top, a slice of *aamshatta* (mango candy) or correct division of biscuits, the aggrieved parties tried to take revenge on me by repeatedly reciting that name; they were often successful. I remember the many tears I'd shed, feeling angry and insulted, on hearing this name in the playground or in the classroom.

The christening was not a sudden affair. There was a bit of history behind it.

On my first day in Brindaban Pundit's primary school, I was dressed in a Shantipur dhoti with an embroidered border and a silk shirt by my maternal grandmother. Undoubtedly, my outfit befitted a newlywed son-in-law arriving at his in-law's house, than a celibate neo-learner attending the abode of his guru. But the dress brought on distress. First, maintaining its position became truly troublesome; then, the end of the carefully pleated, elongated, front part of the dhoti became prone to rolling down on the ground owing to gravity. In one hand, I held a slate and a copy of *Varna Parichaya* by Pt Iswarchandra Vidyasagar and the other hand clutched the ends of the loosened dhoti, somehow made into a confused ball. It looked like a bundle.

The boy named Sidhu, of the Gosains, was the most naughty child in school. He was much older than other learners. A real star in studies, he would be in the same class for a couple of years! Meanwhile, he'd taken up smoking. He came close to me and asked very innocently, 'Boy, what's in that *bonchka* (a bundle, in common parlance), *mudki* or *bataasha*?'

The whole class burst out in laughter. And so Bonchka got off to a start. Any row over a copybook or a pencil invariably stirred up the chant of Bonchka. I'd implored Sidhu so many times, paying him loads of marbles and fix-o-pulls as gratification, to stop him using the name. He pocketed all and assured me, 'Are you crazy? Do I tease you any more? But you are gonna gi'mme that red pencil of yours.'

For that young boy, the sacrifice of that red pencil was no less than the bestowing of the armour by king Karna of the *Mahabharata*. That, too, I conceded; pleaded with him beseechingly, 'See to it, buddy. Please stop the other boys from using that name.'

Wetting the tip of the pencil with his saliva, Sidhu wrote his name in bold letters on a paper and commented lightly, 'Huh, lemme see who has the guts, which son of a- !'

Sidhu, in that tender age, had his vocabulary replete with such a rich collection of chosen expletives that even at this advanced age we're unable to voice them.

But Sidhu didn't care a fig about keeping his word. His record on this count compares favourably with the British Government. The very next day, despite the presence of a teacher in the class, a familiar voice whispered from the back-benches, 'Bonch–' and with it, the sound of muffled laughter from behind slates held to cover faces readily filled the classroom.

Moving closer, I was assured that he was Sidhu, although it's not easy to recognise him. He wore an expensive light grey shark-skin suit; the pair of imported shoes on his feet were as shiny as a mirror. Four rings flashed on two hands, a Parker fifty-one pen and pencil set was tucked in breast-pocket, something which is seen exclusively in possession of the US military commanders in this country. I wondered if it might be the same Sidhu who, only five years ago, used to put up with two others in a dingy ground floor room of a cheap Calcutta hotel at a rent of only one rupee and twelve annas? At that time, he had been serving as a bill collector in an oil mill for a monthly salary of eighteen rupees. It'd have been difficult to identify him as Sidhu without that large black mole beneath his chin.

'What are you doing here? When did you return from London? Have you got married?' Sidhu volleyed the usual threesome.

'We'll come to that later. What about you?'

'I'm fine, executing military contracts these days. By Jove, I'm in money now.' Of course, it needed no clarification.

His story, what I gathered, in brief, is—he'd tried out many vocations after leaving the job in the oil mill. He tried his luck at various odd jobs from selling soaps and detergents, being an agent of one rupee insurance to selling crispy snacks in paper cones. Nothing clicked in his favour. He got into a state when even securing two meals a day became difficult. Then, all of a sudden, the war began.

He found himself a job of overseeing coolies under a contractor who built aerodromes in far-flung areas and left for some forest in Assam. Dame Fortune granted him her favour there. He returned to Calcutta with a bit of capital. He started with the supply of minor items and then settled for bigger contracts. Presently he's in Delhi to liaise with a senior officer of a department.

He was staying at the Swiss Hotel in old Delhi. Reaching there, he took me to his suite. 'You're staying where? Queensway? Well, my vehicle will drop you there. Driver! Wait a while. You have to drop sahib at Queensway.' He spoke with his driver in fluent Hindi, the outcome of overseeing coolies in Assam.

I tried to dissuade him, 'Stop worrying, I'll take a bus.'

'Are you crazy? Buses are too crowded; it shakes the life out of you. Why take so much trouble when a vehicle is there? As it is, I'm paying him hiring charges for the whole day.'

Now it struck me that it was a cab hired for the day. There are no metered taxis in Delhi and their numbers have no 'T' as a prefix. Without prior knowledge, one can't guess if it's a hired vehicle. But it's amazing. Sidhu, of all gentlemen, finds it's hard to commute by bus because it is crowded and it shakes too much! Not long ago, this very Sidhu walked all the way from Pataldanga to Tollygunj under the mid-day sun to see me.

Sidhu ordered the boy to get us whisky. Again, I tried to dissuade him. He answered with a smile, 'You think its from Solan or Mari? This Sidhu boy's tastes are refined enough to not touch those indigenous things! See for yourself, it's original Scotch. Original taste too. Ah, if one has to drink, might as well have the original or it's better to let it be.'

'No, not for that. But where do you get Scotch? I'm told the market's out of … .'

'Yes, it's, not available at the stores; but, of course, there's no shortage in the black market. My brother, it's all about money. Pour it clanking, no dearth of supplies from sons of -.'

I saw it for myself how Sidhu matched his words with action. An orderly was about to return the change of a five rupee note after buying three bottles of soda. 'Thanks. You may keep that.' Sidhu tipped him the entire return very casually. The fellow bowed to the ground and left.

He revealed his reason for visiting Delhi. Back in Calcutta, a junior officer had allegedly lodged a complaint against him and on that complaint, an officer from here would inspect his factory. This had been the cause of his worry.

I failed to appreciate this. What's the harm in there if his factory is inspected?

Sidhu replied annoyed, 'Oh! Had it been there, it could be inspected. But there's none.'

'Then how do you manage to supply your brand?'

'You're still that Bonchka from school. Your stay in England hasn't helped you to strengthen the upper storey with more grey matter! Why need a factory to supply your branded products? Why are there other people's factories? Get it produced there, fix your label and it's done! No stopping by any sons of -. Bit of a printing cost is involved! A few *challan* forms, letterheads, rubber stamps and all these things. Are orders for supplies given on seeing factories? Orders are made...', with these words, he signalled a certain expression in his face and eyes, which seemed partly clear and partly obscure, but together created an enigma!

I asked, 'You have been supplying your items for a long time and no one has enquired about your factory?'

'Why not? Several good reports of inspections have been submitted. It would have been submitted this time too but for that son of a- junior officer? He is too greedy! I can hardly cope with his demands. There's the trouble, you know. Anyway, I'll soon manage to find out everything.'

'How will you find out?'

'Why, the office clerks will help. Won't they? Do you think I'm seeking help gratis? Which damned fool in this world works gratis for others any more? They earn a mere eighty rupees a month; have they even seen five-hundred rupees in their pocket at a time? Let alone information, I've even the knowhow for making files disappear. Oh! Madhubabu! Please come in. What's up? Brother, give me a minute. I'll be right back. This gentleman and I have some private… . Madhubabu, let's go to the veranda.' Sidhu departed with the newcomer.

He returned after twenty minutes and remarked, 'It portends that some fat payments might have to be made. Can't help it, I will have to recover that later.'

I'm long past the stage of wondering. I only queried, 'But will you be able to keep it hidden all along? Won't others in the department discover it?'

'How will they? The gentleman you saw here, he came to pass me the details about the inspecting officer and his itinerary. When I visit his office, will he show any sign of knowing me at all? He will feign that he's never seen me in life. That would take care of everything. Don't all things have a system?'

A bearer brought in a couple of large packets and said, 'Messrs. Phelps has sent it, sir.' Sidhu answered, 'Okay, fine.' He turned to me, 'I went shopping yesterday. That's what they've sent in. Please see the things. You have modern tastes, you know about the latest fashions. Yeah, they're shirts. Only a dozen. Each priced at twenty-six rupees and fifteen annas. You know their technique of pricing with fifteen annas? They would not charge it twenty-seven rupees in full at any cost. Those are handkerchiefs. Yes, it's the pyramid. Rupees seventy a dozen. It suffices that it is at all available; who cares whether seventy a dozen? Or, eighty a dozen? What do they call it? These days the American sahibs often wear it. Is it Darkin? Not Darkin. Then what? Jakin? "A" after "J", right? I can't ask the name of an item in a shop, can I? What will they take me for then?

I bought it on a whim; I'll find an occasion to wear it later. It's not that costly. Rupees two hundred and eighty only. The leather is of good quality.' I saw the bill; with many other sundry items included, it was over seven hundred rupees. He opened his wallet and handed two five-hundred rupee currency-notes to the bearer to pay the bill.

I tried to recollect in silence exactly when before this had I seen him in a shirt not patched.

Sidhu treated me very heartily. It was fascinating to see such generosity towards a childhood friend. It's not difficult to gather from his ways and manners that his bank balance is strong enough to hire my services for ten years! But he wanted me to be his partner instead of an employee. He said, 'So long as you aren't a Barrister and as of now, since the work of a scribe won't fetch you much, why don't you join me? It won't be that bad. It would be of benefit to me also; answering correspondence, talking to sahibs and officers, you know, these are not exactly my forte.'

I said with a wan smile, 'Why bother? As you'd said, those are not really needed for securing orders. Your money will speak for you.'

'You're not far off the mark. Custom rules everywhere. Certainly, to have someone fluent in spoken and written English gives an edge. If you are with me, I can double my income. I'd requested Nityananda. Don't remember him? Well, it's that priest's son, Nitai. Once I tore his sacred thread in our primary school. Thereupon, he stopped using his voice to speak and replied to our questions by moving his hands only. At last, he spoke out loud after taking a loan of a sacred thread from our Sanskrit master. As punishment, I'd had to stand on the bench for two hours as punishment, holding my ears. That Nityananda is now a deputy. For a while, he worked as a supplier also. I told him ways to earn more. He advised me, "Sidhu, as a mischievous boy in school, you created much havoc. As a grown man now, you better don't do it any more!" Hear him once! To earn money, I'm a contractor and you are in service. All that I'm doing is only to add to my income, what mischief is there? I ain't here to chant Lord Hari's name, neither are you.'

Nonetheless, it's a relief. At least a few mortals still exist in this world who haven't fixed their gaze on bank passbooks as the only be-all and end-all of life.

Sidhu continued, 'And what has he gained? His colleague has bought two houses in Lake Road and a car too. His wife displays diamond jewellery. And our Nityananda lives a saint's life, satisfied. He attends office in overcrowded tramcars, dangling like a bat, wears a suit tailored by Wachell Mollah. He's a real dolt, indeed!'

Who dares doubt it!

I asked, 'Well, brother, aren't any remnants of the word honesty found anywhere in this war-driven market any more?'

'Honesty? You mean, always telling the truth, never stealing or cheating? Sorry mate, these good morals which we wrote down in our copies in school—no, it's unfair to say I wrote them; I never really cared to study, I only received caning from our teachers, you all wrote them down—are found in printed books alone. In practical life these are useless. I cross my heart, Bonchka, believe me, there's not a man around who can't be bought off. Only, what matters is the price. A clerk takes a tenner, an accountant settles for two tens and a five, a superintendent for fifty, an inspector takes a hundred. The higher the officer's salary, the higher is his fee. Money can get everything done. But, yes, some do not dare to accept money directly! To them, if it is a European, offer a case of white label; and if a native, gift in a daughter's wedding a Benaras-made silk sari.'

I returned home late in the night, dropped by Sidhu Chandra's hired vehicle, after having dinner with him. He'd stuffed my cigarette case with 'Black and White' cigarettes. It's scarce now in the 'white' market, but is it so in the 'black'? Does our country have any dearth of Sidhu Chandras?

Eleven

The authors of our Shashtras have prescribed that visiting the monarch is an act of virtue. It's not known though if visiting a counsellor of the king brings virtue as well. Or else, why would a crowd gather daily in the bungalows of the executive councillors? The members of the crowd are not ordinary folks, they're ICS officers.

In the grassy and spacious lawns facing the elegant bungalow of an executive councillor, the master of the house takes a seat for a tête-à-tête in the afternoon. A telephone on a tripod near his chair is connected to the plug point in his private secretary's room via a long wire. The secretary connects the calls to his boss's telephone, through a switch, depending on who is calling and what the conversation is about. About a dozen cane chairs spray-painted with green valspar enamel are placed in front. Using wooden chairs in the garden is not considered aristocratic. The evening assemblies of the ICS-encircled councillors remind one of the retinue of planets that revolve around the sun. These are the daily durbars of the councillors of the king. Albeit, a durbar for the rich, not for the enriched.

They don white satiny denim trousers and half-sleeve shirts. No tie, no coat. This is the dress code of New Delhi in summer. This is for all occasions, from attending office to dinner. The young put on a sport-shirt in lieu of a shirt. It looks even smarter. On socks-free feet they wear white Kabuli slippers. Like khakis in the army, the civilians too have a uniform which though not guided by any writ is a by an unwritten code of fashion; as is wont for the members of the groom's party in a Bengali wedding to wear finely pleated dhotis and gold-buttoned *punjabi*s. The ICS officers of all origins and regions of the country, wear the same dress and speak the same language. Obviously, neither of the two—the outfit or the language—shares its origin with the user's place of birth.

The person, using whose assistance I could enter into these seas of meetings, is a high official in the government. A man, well-known for his savoir faire, advanced in age, unmarried and very generous. There are very few houses which have not seen him in even fewer hostesses who do not invite him to dinner parties.

All men without a mate become maniacal about something or the other; either it is playing-cards or theatre or avowed determination serve the country well or literature or a swamiji. This man is maniacal about his clothes. He is known as the best dressed man in New Delhi. Rumour has it that once he was required to go on a tour for four days all of a sudden. Being in haste and not finding enough time to take adequate clothes, he had to rush out with only two wardrobe trunks and a suitcase. These contained fifteen suits, one and a half dozen shirts, ten ties and twenty handkerchiefs! Nobody has ever seen him in shirts not freshly ironed, or in trousers without creases. Laundrymen regularly visit his home in the morning to press bedclothes, pillow-covers, sleeping suits and other clothes. His friends advise him to keep an electric iron in the office so that before attending to the call of his boss, he could do a last-minute ironing of the shirt he wears.

The gentleman is attentive about his clothes but not attached to them. Very casually, he often distributes elegant-looking neckties and lovely mufflers among his cronies. Unflinching hospitality is the way in his home. We do not often meet such an affable person.

He is one of those few Indians who suffer from no soft corner for the sahibs. Once, on his way to Bombay, he was changing trains at a station in the middle of the night. An Englishman was sleeping in a first class compartment, locked from inside. Driven by repeated knocks and calls, the sahib opened the door with much annoyance and found but a native at the door. Sahib screamed at him, '*Vaago*' and again locked the door with a bang. But this native was made of a different mould, he did not hold sahibs in awe. The station master sought to solve the problem by accommodating him in a different bogey, but he wouldn't budge. The sahib hadn't reserved the entire compartment, so he most certainly would travel in that very compartment.

It's nothing unusual for the sahib to lose patience at this. Imagine the audacity of the native; he might be a man with money and a first class ticket, but how dare he think of travelling in the same compartment with a pure-bred English sahib! My god, what's happened to India? Is that half-naked rodent 'Gyandi' the Viceroy in Delhi now? Is Willingdon gone? The sahib brandished his whip and blocking the door, said, 'You see this?'

The gentleman took out a revolver from his pocket and said, 'See this?'

The sahib looked at him agape and quickly disappeared from the door to lie down on his berth.

Though sahibs wield lathis on this sort of strong-willed men as police officers, send them to prisons as magistrates, but despite this, they bear deep respect in their minds for them. For such men alone, we may unhesitatingly introduce ourselves as Indians in a foreign land.

A colonel in the army was his superior for some time. He had spent long years reprimanding Punjabi havaldars and sepoys. Once, the colonel applied this method on him, thinking this was the only means of getting work done by an Indian. The calm reply came forthwith to the colonel, 'Colonel, this is not how you speak to an officer. Please remember, if you shout like that, I can shout back too.'

I've been told that this colonel, at a later time, often invited him to dinner in his house, conveyed, in person, 'Get well soon' messages whenever he was ill and at the time of retirement, recommended his promotion by praising him profusely.

We entered the arena of the evening meeting of an executive councillor in the middle of the discourse. My friend introduced me to the master of the house and his courtiers. Uniformed bearers served delicious drinks in beautiful glasses and expensive cigarettes from silver cases. The master of the house is a chain smoker. He picks up and passes cigarettes, one after another, to his lips. There seems to be a contest running as to who might be the first to light it by striking a match. A Europe-returned enjoys a place of eminence in this country. Moreover, if he is attached to a European newspaper, then it's paramount. The excessive nature of the welcome and amiability of the hon'ble members of the Executive Council of His Highness, the Governor-General of India, marked this visit.

Following the lead of the ongoing discourse, it was revealed that the subject of discussion was the excessive heat of summer in New Delhi. Akin to the annual chariot festival of Lord Jagannath, the government of India also has an annual festival of sojourn to the hills. In early April, the departments are transferred to the hills of Simla. In autumn, like the return chariot festival, those are again reverted to Delhi. Twice-a-year, a procession of cartloads of trunks, boxes and other dead stock is seen on the Cart Road in Simla and on Paharganj Road in New Delhi. This year, first time ever, transit to the hills has been put off by order of the government.

The newly appointed, temporary Commander-in-Chief, General Molseworth, has vetoed this year's sojourn in Simla. If our soldiers can fight the Japanese in the simmering heat of the woods and forests of Burma, why might not the civilian sahibs in the Secretariat bear with a little heat? Winning a war demands hardships.

The writ of the army's need is overriding. So, that has to be accepted, although with reluctance. The Secretary-Sahibs are unnerved; it's so hot already by the end of this March! How much more searing it would be in May–June!

Most of the deputy secretaries are Indian. So they took a lead over others and said, 'It would be horrible! We've got to run off the place on medical leave in May–June.'

Their wives are still more severe. In the afternoons, when the husbands are away in office, they whisper, 'Have you heard the advice of the new Commander-in-Chief? We're staying back in Delhi this summer. My goodness! Rather, we women could stay together as though in a mess in Simla and let our men stay in Delhi to be boiled in the summer heat.'

The Executive Councillor asked, 'Does it get too hot here in summer?'

One answered readily, 'Severe! You can't even stay here.'

Another said, 'Many get affected by boils appearing all over in the heat.'

The third said, 'The *loo* will be blowing in from April.' *Loo* is the strong, hot and dry summer wind which blows from the west.

The Executive Councillor said, 'Well, you see, the Secretariat rooms are all air-conditioned. We'll have to spend the afternoon there. Somehow we've got to manage.'

The fourth man, who was uneasy heretofore, finding nothing to add to the conversation, readily seconded the idea, 'Of course, it can be managed. Don't people stay in Delhi in summer?'

The Executive Councillor said, staring at him, 'And the *loo* won't blow in every night, will it?'

He added excitedly, 'As you said, sir. It's always cool after dark. Besides, a room in each HM bungalow will be air-conditioned. It'll be tolerable, I believe.'

'HM' stands for Hon'ble Member or Minister. The executive councillors are known in the government circle by that name.

The first speaker, who was elaborating so far on excessive hotness, was palpably down. He should have uttered the words of the fourth man. He felt a pang in his heart and was almost angry with this fourth respondent. He mused, 'Only flattery! The moment HM said that the summer heat was to be managed somehow, he was all-effort to prove as though the heat is nothing serious! A real humbug! I'm sure, had HM not preferred to stay on in Delhi, he would have said the opposite!' He felt much relieved, assuring himself that the man was of a shameless flatterer type, which he himself never was.

HM changed the topic from summer heat to the work of the government. Anecdotes of the council and its background. Flowery accounts elaborating on how his English colleagues' wiles to establish British interests get prevented by his efforts, or, where and when his sharp farsightedness had firmly secured interests of the country in the government.

It was apparent that the listeners were already convinced. They were unanimous in agreement even before his submissions. A few there expressed deep concern conjecturing the possible perils of poor Mother India, had HM not been there. They were almost on the verge of tears.

Talking about the country, the long arm of inter-connectedness brought forth words on the Congress. Condemning severely the barren policy of the Congress leadership, HM said, 'Walking into jails alone won't give us freedom.' Although he didn't vent clearly exactly what would give us freedom, no misgiving remained as to the assertion that only efforts of the executive councillors can deliver it. Even on this, the assembly held complete unanimity.

HM said that he cared not to think much and took decisions on the spur of the moment. Readily, an approval floated, 'Sir, much thought has been spent in connection with our land. Now it's time to jump into action.'

HM corrected him, 'Of course, it's not wise to act out on something all of a sudden, without thinking about it.'

'No doubt about it, Sir, acting without thinking is foolhardiness,' glibly remarked that same man.

After acknowledging an invitation to a dinner next week and bidding farewell to HM, we exited onto the street. My companion said that a friend of his had named this assembly of skilled bootlickers anew as Flunkey's Foundation. An apt name, indeed!

It's not difficult to get at the heart of it. They are ICS officers; in the terminology of the native press, belonging to the 'heaven-born' service. Like the chastity of Caesar's wife, their competence is beyond all questions. Their future is unhindered and their power defies limits. They are well-versed in all scriptures. That's why one who is the assistant collector of an unknown sub-division in Bihar today, becomes the Chairman of Karachi Port Trust tomorrow, the Controller of Broadcasting the day after, the Director-General of Archaeology on the morrow and the Agricultural Commissioner the following day. They know, by heart, that keeping executive councillors in good humour begets fast promotions. So they arrive with their wives to take HM to a movie, else, they invite him to a dinner, or, attend to him on each halves of a day to deliver their best 'yes-sirs'. To be a member of the Flunkey Foundation, one need not pay any fees; they need only attend the right place.

The Indian Civil Service is a wonderful creation of the British administration. Its members number around eleven hundred, and almost half are Indians. This service is an ideal example of procuring supporters of imperialism from amongst the very citizens of a subjugated nation. The British Government attracts bright students of universities by offering inflated pay and an attractive pension. By selecting the best specimens from among youths and employing them in administration, the administration confirms the country's slavery, makes poverty ever-escalating and makes the national movement fraught with danger.

An extraordinary infatuation marks the three letters of the English alphabet, I C S. These three letters at the end of a European's name suggests that the man was a student of a public school, passed out from Oxford or Cambridge and has qualified in a very difficult competitive examination. It emphasises the fact that he has knowledge of an Indian language, has received an overseas allowance, started as an assistant collector and will end up either as an executive councillor or as a provincial governor. It also states that he has started at five hundred rupees and will end at six or eight thousand, he will be superannuated at the age of sixty with one thousand sterling-pounds as pension and a home in England or the Riviera, will enjoy a peaceful retired life and certainly bear in mind a strong apathy towards India.

If an Indian, it would mean that he is noble born, with good results in the college, beyond the suspicion of the police, untouched by swadeshi, has lead an impeccable student life, has dedication towards Occidentalism and in service, wholeheartedly given to the achievements of the executive departments over the judiciary. For them lies waiting, cosy chairs in a public puja pandal, chairmanship in the prize distribution ceremony of a school, opportunities to publish inane pieces in monthly magazines and the ardent sighs of anxious mothers of nubile daughters.

In common parlance, they are called the framework of British rule in India–the 'Steel Frame'. There were and still are, among them, a few who through their learning, genius and industry could be the pioneer in any academic field. They translated the *Rig Veda*, critically analysed the economy of British India, authored the first complete *History of India*, created wonderful literature, introduced the co-operative movement and above all, founded the Indian National Congress. Surendranath, the guru of Nationalism, Rishi Aurobindo and Subhas Chandra, the rebel, quit this service either after being or in the process of being a part of it.

But, exceptions prove the rule. Most of the members of the ICS are mediocre. All that they write are files, read are gazettes and discuss are about furloughs, promotions or retirements. Their ultimate ambitions constitute the knighthood for themselves at the end, a Buick car for their wives and imperial service for their sons.

They say that gold costs less than cannon. The infallible weapon to resist the grievance of the educated against foreign rule is to make them an integral part of the administrative machinery. An amount of twenty-five million rupees is spent annually from the revenue of India for the eleven hundred members of the ICS. On an average, an ICS rules over an area of eight-hundred and sixty-eight square miles comprising two and a half lakh people. They are elevated to a special class as a consequence of being lavished with money, having an enviable career and playing a lead role in foreign affairs. They are unencumbered by a sense of responsibility for the country and are dissociated from the common touch of countrymen. ICS is not a profession; it is a race of its own kind. The Holy Roman Empire was neither holy, nor Roman, nor worthy of the name empire; the Indian Civil Service is, likewise, neither Indian, nor civil, nor has an iota of the spirit of service in it.

Twelve

Sir Stafford Cripps quit Delhi.[3]

The previous evening, through a radio message from Delhi Radio, he addressed the citizens of India, announcing and explaining the failure of Cripps Mission. I guess, other than Weakham Stead, the ex-editor of *London Times*, there is no match in the British Empire for Cripps as a radio commentator. His manner of speaking is peerless and so is his voice. It's a matter of regret that he unjustly applied his skills in maligning India, in particular, the Congress party. His radio lecture will go down in history as one of the choicest examples of political infamy on account of wilful distortion, suppression of facts, baseless allegations, contradictory remarks and misleading arguments.

The entire lecture smacked of an arrogant disdain towards the weak, of the bruised ego of a power-conscious haughty man. The tone of the voice of Sir Stafford had that hint of ire which a spurned well-to-do donor feels towards his self-possessed disadvantaged relative for refusing to accept his hand-outs of pity-mixed alms.

Cripps said that he was here to play neutral mediator through the good offices of the British Government, to resolve the serious differences that existed among the different political parties in India. The listeners rubbed eyes in disbelief; were we listening to a lecture by Adolf Hitler? He, too, claimed that he was always for peace!

Those who have engendered communal divisions in this country by means of resorting to ways such as government job allocations, separate electorates, political favouritism and so on and have been careful to sustain differences of opinion, are now playing the role of a mediator! Could anything be more farcical?

Cripps said that all reasonable men would agree that in this portentous hour of the war, it's not feasible to compose a new instrument for governance. As though the Indian leadership had failed to acknowledge this. All that they wanted was formation of an ad-hoc national government with true powers vested in it, as it was the most strongly felt need of this dark hour. The demand of the popular leaders was to give recognition to the National Government, drawn from the top leadership of the country, as an equivalent of the cabinet of ministers of an independent country and through an unwritten rule, the Governor-General would act only as the titular head with no power to veto the recommendations of the National Government.

The Congress was at the receiving end of most of the fury. He said that Congress sought to usurp the powers of governing the country, almost dictatorially, as the party with the majority in the National Government. Woe is me! Maulana Azad wrote in a letter to Cripps on eleventh April that the Congress was willing to form a National Government in coalition with other political parties. All the deliberations were based on this. The size of the National Government and proportion of representation of different political parties in it could very well be the items of dialogues at an appropriate stage. The Congress was not attempting to usurp power for itself; its demand was the transmission of genuine power of governance to the hands of the Indians.

As an objection to vesting the portfolio of national defence in the hands of an Indian, Cripps said that Britain had the responsibility of defending India and it was not possible for Britain to back out from the duty it had towards the allied powers. To meddle with the power of the supreme commander of the military during the war would not help in realising victory. The president of the Congress party had clearly said that the Congress had no intention to interfere with the war operations of the supreme commander. On the contrary, they were ready to entrust more control in him if the minister of defence was an Indian. But the ultimate control in the defence of the country must be vested in the hands of a representative of the country. Else, independence is a farce.

General McArthur of USA is the supreme allied commander for South-east Asia in the fight against the Japanese. Despite that, the defence secretary of Australia is an Australian, not an American or an Englishman; this was cited as an example by some. But there is no instance where the British Government can be seen to show any regard for logical arguments.

His most ridiculous remark was on the subject of the accountability of the National Government. He said, 'The Congress intends to form a national government over which the Governor-General or the British Government will have no control. Let's spare a few thoughts on what this means. The Indian government will then be formed by a few men who will not be answerable to any legislature or an electorate and will be removable by none.' How awful! Really, one certainly can't allow this to happen! The only pure and original specimen of a government which is accountable to a combination of the legislature, electorate and people and can be removed is our present day Benthal-Maxwell-Noon-Osman-Ramswami encircled government-in-power of the most gracious Lord Linlithgow!

In the conclusion of the radio lecture, Cripps made many impassioned remarks, with a view to egg on India's resistance against the Japanese onslaught, 'We'll have to take risks, try new methods, rise above old mindsets' and so forth.

Sir Stafford enjoys the renown of an unrivalled barrister. But what surprises one is how the inherent weaknesses and incongruities of all these remarks fell out of his sight. 'We'll have to take risks'. It's true. But it is not so for the British Government but for the dependant, oppressed Indian masses. 'We'll try new methods!' But still the old autocracy will remain in place in India. 'We'll have to rise above old mindsets'. Except in the Indian context!

This is the gospel of Sir Stafford Cripps, Britain's most progressive socialist indophile!

That a temporary national government on the model of the War Cabinet of Britain would be formed was the basis on which Maulana Azad and Pt Nehru deliberated upon Cripps' proposals. It was revealed later that the British authority would not budge from the concept of a second edition of the Viceroy's Executive Council. Cripps didn't even acknowledge in his radio broadcast that he'd even hinted at the concept of a national government in any deliberations ever. In that case, none but the rabid or the motivated would perhaps believe that Maulana Azad and Pt Nehru had spent three weeks discussing reconstruction of the Executive Council or joining it.

The president of Congress stated emphatically that Cripps had assured them of a national government. Cripps denied it straightaway. Even though all the reporters who were present on twenty-third March in the press conference would also testify that Cripps had talked about this national government there as well.

The Congress leadership has committed a fatal error. They have not preserved any written and unanimously accepted document of Cripps' deliberations. I've seen merchants in England prepare mutually agreed upon scripts of parties' discussions on a particular trade-off or trade-pact. Following the conclusion of a discussion, one party prepares a draft of the minutes and sends it to the other. The other either accepts it or proposes corrections to it. This arrangement attempts to rectify the errors of misconstruing the other in the course of oral deliberations. This certainly displays an unbelievable childish absence of forethought on the part of the Congress authorities, that they had not taken any such precautions, especially when the outcome of the discussions involved the fate of four hundred million Indians. Had the substance of the day's discussions been recorded on the same evening in a register duly authorised by a signature of Cripps, then the tirade accusing each other of falsifying facts wouldn't have taken place.

Maulana Azad wrote in his letter, 'the more the deliberation between Congress and Cripps advances, the greater the gradual deterioration in the British.' This comment is not unfounded. Cripps' character seems to have undergone a sea change in the gap between his arrival with the proposals from Britain and his departure from India.

Cripps' failure, as well as his change of heart are open to research and informed guesswork. The entire onus of the failure, naturally, is not his.

It's not difficult to presume that Lord Linlithgow didn't wish for any success to the Cripps Mission. He'd tried in vain earlier to garner the support of the Indian masses for the war against the Japanese. So it was not at all desirable for him to see the success in somebody else's efforts to achieve a goal in which he had failed miserably, especially when that somebody is a member of the Labour party. It's not unknown to anyone that Lord Linlithgow is a diehard Conservative.

There is neither any means to know if Archibald Wavell, the commander-in-chief of the Allies, had the willingness to work under an Indian defence secretary. Wavell is now Britain's most lauded military commander. The British Government places unwavering faith on his war strategies. In no case will it accept any defence proposal on India sans his stamp of approval.

The popular belief is that Sir Stafford Cripps was cautioned from London over the telephone to not exercise any discretion beyond the written proposals of the War Cabinet. This can't be ruled out in the context of the well-known attitude of Churchill and Emery towards India.

At the beginning of the Second World War, Cripps was indistinguishable in the political arena of England. He was then estranged from the Labour party too. He came to India in the last quarter of 1939. He visited many places, interacted closely with different Indian leaders, as a guest of Pt Jawaharlal Nehru he researched on this country's national movement and its diverse forms.

Cripps travelled to China from India. The Chamberlain government had fallen by the time he returned to England from China via Russia. A new coalition government was formed with Churchill as the Prime Minister. The diplomatic relation between Britain and Russia was then not at all cordial, but resisting Hitler in Europe was possible only by befriending Russia. Who would take this responsibility? It's not possible to find out who proposed Cripps' name. But one day, all of a sudden, Cripps, almost forgotten in political circles, entered 10 Downing Street casting aside his fabulous income from his successful legal practice. Churchill might have told him, 'You like Moscow. Please go there as our ambassador. You have to establish cordial relations between Britain and Russia. Start right now, for God's sake!'

Cripps went to Russia and achieved the well-nigh impossible objective. He managed to thaw the ice between Britain and Russia. His fame and popularity was sky-high when he returned in 1942, after completing his assignments in Moscow and Kuybyshev. Churchill received him in the War Cabinet.

Cripps believed he would be able to find a satisfactory solution to the India problem. Didn't he know that the proposals of the War Cabinet fell far too short to meet India's national aspirations? It raises doubt over his well-advertised keen intelligence. The popular belief is that Gandhi asked Cripps on the very first meeting, 'Why are you here with these proposals?' He had advised him, 'If you are unable to concede more than these, you may as well take a return flight home.'

Cripps surely knew that the proposals of the War Cabinet did not suffice. But he gambled on the strength of his personal good relations with the Indian leaders that somehow he would be able to achieve their concurrence. But Congress leaders are not mere children; they did not let personal preferences dominate the choice of fate of the nation.

Perhaps Cripps had speculated that he, as the person on the spot, would have some leeway with regard to the proposals and manoeuvre them somewhat on behalf of the British Government. Churchill frustrated him. He suffered a broken heart on both counts.

One who is firm on his ideals and is honest might have resigned from the ministry, announcing publicly that India's demands are justifiable; the sincerity of the British Government is questionable and not conducive to amicable settlement. Cripps didn't go for this. He made caustic comments about the Congress, in support of the British Government. At this extremely critical time for Britain, he chose to trade truth and justice for support and loyalty in favour of his leader and colleagues in the British Government. He falsified his words for the sake of Great Britain's needs. Sir Stafford Cripps, the socialist, committed suicide, to serve the need of the empire.

Churchill won. Not only in the effort to keep India subjugated but he also gained victory over his own possible political rival.

The people of England were not happy with the premiership of Churchill. One after another defeats in the diverse battlefields everywhere had much moved the members of the Parliament. They voiced bitter criticism towards the inability of the Churchill Government. But they didn't remove him. It was not out of regard or faith in his leadership. They were completely undone because there was no other person in England worthy to be the premier.

The fame and respect Cripps had won in his unforeseen success in Russia had brought on him popular attention.According to the grapevine, Sir Stafford Cripps would be the future Prime Minister of England. Had he been able to solve the Indian problem satisfactorily, the faith of the British people in Cripps's abilities would have grown deeper and in politics, his unmatched influence would rival Churchill. Churchill sent Cripps to India as an emissary of the War Cabinet's hollow proposals, which he knew for sure that Gandhi, Azad and Nehru would not accept at any cost.

Cripps failed in his mission. Churchill's leadership remained safe. There are several ways to remove rivals in politics. Stalin finished them with bullets; Churchill checkmated them by diplomatic manoeuvres. Socialist Cripps, hand in hand with imperialist Tories, signed unawares his own death warrant in British politics.

I had an invitation for dinner at a friend's house. The gentleman belongs to the covenant service of a renowned British firm in Calcutta—the only native member in an all-white board of directors. He enjoyed enviable pay and abundant say. For urgent war related works the Government has appointed him in the Supply Department with even higher pay. He retains a lien in his company. When the war is over he will join back his company.

The number of invitees was around ten and among them, only I was single. All others who arrived were married couples. Dinner would be served at 9:00 pm but by half past seven all invitees arrived. The drawing-room resonated with the sounds of laughter and mirth.

The difference between our old form of feasting and this sort of evening soiree is distinct. This distinction is not localised only in seating arrangements and the use of knives and forks. Our traditional feasts have a relation mainly with social functions in its varying reincarnations. Invitees there are mostly kinsmen, irrespective of whether there is a cordiality with them or not. So the number defies count. Under the awning on the rooftop where the meal is to be served, rows of seventy or eighty invitees sit at a time. Ladies are accommodated in the bedrooms, after removing the four-poster bed or the cot. Even this does not finish feeding the guests in one go. The cacophony is audible from a quarter of a mile!

English-style dinner invitation needs no special occasion, nor any specific date. The host has no abiding obligation to invite any particular person. 'Hostess' should be more appropriate actually because it is the ladies who send the invitations out.

The practice of sitting together at a table restricts the number to six or a maximum of twelve. That includes the lord of the house and his lady. She does not occupy herself in the pantry to oversee the proper kneading of the dough; she is a participant in the discussions at the drawing room like other invitees. Her clothes are not turmeric-smeared, her face is not pale due to an exposure to the oven fire and she is not weary of serving guests. She, too, is elegantly dressed and ornamented. She is not the last to sit and eat at an hour in the late afternoon when all the guests have been served. She joins her guests. The master of the house keeps a watchful eye on the treatment of the guests even as he sits together with the invitees and does not busy himself with a salt pot in hand.

Dining to the fill is not the sole objective of an English dinner party. It's an occasion for friends to get together. So the arrangement is rather frugal. Anything less than ten varieties of curries and five kinds of sweetmeat would not invite criticism here. Competing on the number of *pantua*s speeding down the gullet is not a feature of an English-style dinner. Those who tirelessly research the faults in our Anglican-Bengali modern society may well be grateful to us about this.

Our host is a sociable type. He is capable of jazzing up a party. Game hunting was his hobby once. He narrated episodes of hunting sambar in the forests of Bihar and leopard in the jungles of Assam.

His card tricks are excellent. He surprised us all by taking out, blindfolded, the jack of clubs from a deck of cards, changing a nine of hearts to the jack in a flash by turning his hand and then, he took out the king of spades from the folds of the sari of a lady invitee which earned him a coy chastisement from her and requests of encore from others. Bearers served cold drinks and tomato-juice in cocktail glasses as the party proceeded through fun and frolic.

Dinner was laid in an adjacent room; buffet-style dinner. All the diverse items were arranged on a table in a row. The menu included roast, salad, chops and side-by-side, paratha, biriyani, stuffed gourd. Pudding and *rosogolla* were both present. There was nothing to wonder about the arrangement as it was representative of our thought, work, speech and clothes: a mix of cultures. A wristwatch worn with a xylophonic array of bangles on a female hand is common view, so is a double-cuffed shirt above plaited dhoti donned by men.

Plates are arranged one above another on one side of the sideboard and spoons, forks and knives are kept at the other end. It is customary to help oneself by taking one's picks on one's plate. Men usually partake of their food, standing around the table. Women take a chair or follow the custom of men. The hostess takes care of guests while she helps herself. She insists, 'Why is it so? Mili, you aren't really taking anything. Mr Sen, please take one more chop. Have you tried the roast, Mrs Desai?'

I'd heard of Mrs Saha's name before, but saw her first here in this dinner party. She is ultra slim and much blonder than the average Bengali girls. Her excessive make up has hidden the natural complexion of her cheeks so much that her white-as-paper face seemed to suggest that she was convalescing after a profound illness and had just returned from a sanatorium in the hills. She wears a very expensive, milky white and almost transparent-as-glass chiffon sari. Her light coloured inner was visible through it. A border on a sari is not modern enough now. The pair of slender arms hung from the puffed sleeves of her blouse. Her V-cut front of the blouse painfully exposes the two stark collar bones. A pearl necklace adorns her neck. A pair of danglers, inlaid resplendently with many mustard-seed pearl pieces, almost touched her shoulders. On her long and lean left ring-finger, she wears a matching outsize pearl-set ring. She stands out completely in her dress and ornamental gear among the assembled women wearing saris in green, blue, maroon or violet. She seemed like a tallish stalk of tuberose amidst the colourful flowerbeds in a garden in winter.

The lady served herself half a tablespoon of biriyani, which she carried around as though it was impossible for her to finish off. The hostess made an attempt to serve a bit of roast onto her plate. 'I can't, I can't, please don't,' she pleaded. After much persuasion she took a chop and partook a quarter of it very cautiously by her two manicured fingers. She insisted, 'I'm awfully full. I can't eat any more.'

There was a hot preparation of chilli pepper on the table, of which Mrs Saha picked up some on her plate. It's in vogue. Mr Saha warned her, 'Stop trying that. It's too hot and might make you fall ill.' This too was a cliché. Husbands warn their wives not to consume chillies and wives ignore that to consume more of it, underlining that this is the latest gastronomic delight of the ladies.

After dinner was over, the assembled ladies were requested to sing songs. Some kept up the request; some avoided it by saying they'd been 'out of practice for a long while'. The hostess sings in a manner of speaking and she needn't be pressed much to perform. A Gujarati lady sang songs in her native tongue. One of her songs was composed by the devotee poet Narasingha Mehta. His composition, 'Vaishnava janato teney kahi', has earned much fame as a favourite of Mahatma Gandhi.

Mrs Saha is generous. The dinner party ended very late into the night. She offered me a ride in her car to my place of abode. She said to Mr Saha, 'Biren, you have to drop Minisahib on Queensway'.

Ultra-moderns address their husbands by their names. It's mimicking the English. I'm not an orthodox. I've no faith in the doctrinal explanation that to address the husband by his name is forbidden for a woman. But, I find nothing about it to be thrilled with pleasure if our wives set out to call us as Sudhir, Vikas, or Upen, like John, Arthur or Cyril in English.

If names had no other use than identification, then using numbers, instead of names, would have sufficed the purpose easily. Then, nursing mothers wouldn't have been worried about selecting names for their newborn daughters. Then, poet Rabindranath wouldn't be flooded with request-letters to invent ever newer names for the newborns.

For inert objects, a name is only indicative of it. That naming a rose by any other prosaic name wouldn't change its fragrance is known to one and all like it was known to Shakespeare; but it's a truism that this naming has the potential to banish something from the perimeter of poetic and romantic thought.

But human identity is not confined to any particular expression of being. In different circumstances, for different reasons, to different persons, identity of men takes different forms. To articulate that one enjoys different names. To the officialdom, one who is known as Mr Mukherjee, to his friends in the locality he is Binodbabu, to his classmates in primary schools, he is Bindé, to his mother at home he is 'Khokon' and to a very particular person he is 'Da'ling' or an interjectional variant of it in native dialect, '*Ogo*' or '*Suncho*' or '*Ai*'. These are not only names but indicators as well; more of a symbol than a definition. To a particular man these sounds carry a special connotation, as though, special tunes resonate to a special ear. Seasoned men know that the able ones can be a victor, can blossom a bud, with these little phonic symbols.

Thirteen

I guess every man experiences a vulnerable time in his life when his heart takes precedence over his head. Those moments appear all of a sudden, like a gusty wind and tear open the ties of fortitude of over-cautious people. At that, abstemious yogis stray from their aims, calculative usurers misplace entries in book-keeping and reticent, contemplative people become so moved that they even open their mind to others. In a similar vulnerable moment, the past history of Mr Adharkar came to light quite unexpectedly. The underlying mystery of his meditative, tired eyes and solitary living was exposed in his own words.

A shred of cloud had appeared on the north-eastern sky in the afternoon. We, the heat-stricken band of miserables, expected a shower. It didn't rain, it stormed blindingly. A dust storm. Only seeing can convince one of its form. Bengal has never witnessed this. One cannot imagine from where such a demonic rush of huge clusters of dust comes in, blackening the sky and the world around. An even darker cover of dust blankets the sun. One has to switch on the light at daytime in a room. Even if doors and windows are sealed, some dust invades the eyes and the nostrils, invades clothes within closed trunks. Not a trace of rain, a storm of only dry dust fills the air. But by this blinding storm, temperature dips considerably, the earth cools down. This is a wonderful natural phenomenon in North India.

We sat face to face in a closed room. The storm blew outside, amassing dust everywhere. Adharkar narrated his own life-history in a low tone and at a slow pace.

The profession of Adharkar's ancestors was warfare. His forefathers had fought the Mughals, clashed with Yashwant Singh. His great-grandfather Vishnudutt was a general in the army of Peshwa Bajirao. In the battle of Asai he fought right beside the Peshwa and destroyed enemies by his matchless might. He fell to a bullet that hit him in the chest. Adharkar saw in his boyhood the blood-stained armour of his great-grandfather, the family's carefully preserved glorious inheritance. He carries the valour of a hero in his blood.

His family possessed abundant wealth, ample fame, but were not exposed to modern education. Adharkar was the only son of his father and was sent to an English school in Poona. He went to Manchester after passing out from Elphinstone College. When he returned after obtaining his degree in textile engineering, the First World War had ended in Europe. He established a cloth mill in Bombay and worked monstrously hard to make it a success.

Five years passed by. One evening he went to Dadar station, awaiting the arrival of a friend. His friend didn't turn up. As he was returning, he caught a female voice saying something. It was too mellifluous to ignore. He didn't make out what she said though. He looked around and saw a young lady on the platform, accompanying a middle-aged man. Suitcases, hold-alls, wicker baskets and so on were kept piled in front of them. The signs of anxiety were marked on their faces. At that instant, uncontrolled rampage and arson by communal rioters was rife in Bombay. Railway passengers were harrassed by the paucity of porters inside the station and a lack of hired carriages outside. Stepping out of home after dark was not safe.

Adharkar asked them, 'Have you come to Bombay for the first time?' The gentleman replied, 'Yes, a relative of mine stays here. I'd sent him a wire asking him to be present in the station. He hasn't come. It seems he hasn't received it after all.'

'Even if he received it, reaching here is difficult. Riots have broken out in the town. Arson and killings are rampant. Where do you want to go?'

'Well, I'm in a fix then. Can you suggest a hotel in the vicinity?'

'Yes, of course. But you won't get accommodation there. The staff in most hotels have left fearing for their lives. The few boarders who are still there are running short of water and other provisions. Hotels are not admitting new guests.'

'What will we do then?' The gentleman looked at his companion. She was shaken, her countenance had turned pale. An attempt to accommodate them in the waiting room of the station fell through. There was no room. All spaces were already occupied with long-distance travellers. The woman looked at her husband in utter helplessness.

Adharkar proposed, 'If you don't mind, you may come to my flat. Tomorrow morning we can look for your relative. I've got my car waiting.'

The gentleman looked at his wife. She hesitatingly spoke in English to her husband; unmistakably, the target of her words was Adharkar, 'It would be very bothersome for his wife if we reach his home unexpectedly in the night.'

That melody repeated again. Perhaps this was the tone of Padmini, the wife of Bhim Singh, which inspired the Rajput youth to lay down their life in battle; perhaps Helen of Troy also had this quality which took thousands of men-of-war to the sea.

Adharkar said, 'I'm not sure if accommodating helpless guests for a night in home amounts to botheration to a wife, maybe it's so. But, you can be easy in the mind, my wife would not be bothered at all, because I've none.'

'You've got no...? Oh, then…', the woman halted her speech midway.

'Then, what?' Adharkar asked.

'We're grateful to you. We can spend the night somehow on the platform.'

'Oh, I forgot! To be a guest in a bachelor's home is not really socially acceptable, no? Then you stay on the platform. What's there to fear? I don't see the Goan coolies now, but they must be somewhere around. You wear jewelled ornaments; you have belongings worth several hundreds of rupees. They won't last long. Send a line to me tomorrow morning in case there's the need to identify the dead. Good night, then.' Adharkar strode out of the place in a huff. His voice was full of ire.

Curiously, Adharkar was found back on the scene in five minutes. 'I've an idea', he said. 'Let's go to my flat. After reaching there, I'll spend the night in one of my clerk's residences nearby. Then my home will be cleared of the blemish of bachelorhood. Bolt it well from inside, however; that would be safer than this platform, I guess.'

The woman was frightened at the mention of Goan coolies. The husband too was not much in favour of the idea of spending the night on the platform. So they agreed to his proposal. No porter could be found. Adharkar lent a hand in carrying the two large suitcases to his car with whistling ease.

It was a small flat; only one bedroom. As Adharkar raised himself to move out after dinner, the woman asked him in clear English, 'How odd! Where are you going?'

'To my clerk's place?'

'To your clerk's place? How far is that?'

'About five miles.'

'At this late hour in the night? Do you have any special business there?'

'The business of spending the night.'

'Why, what's wrong with this house?'

Adharkar was not ready for this. He fumbled, 'No, nothing wrong, er, but if you feel uneasy…'

The woman intervened in an impatient voice, 'Who told you that? And even if it is so, how can you take us for uncivilised people who drive the shelter-giver out of his own home in a riot-troubled night for their own comfort? Better still you ask us to leave for the platform!'

The husband added forcefully, 'Are you crazy? Going out at this hour of the night?'

Another round of arguments ensued about the sleeping arrangement. There was only one cot. Adharkar wanted his guests to sleep on it and he would sleep on the floor of the drawing room. The guests wished just the opposite. But, this time too, the lady won.

Adharkar remarked on his way to the bedroom, 'Too bad. You must be blaming me helluva lot that I'm way too fussy, leaving guests on the floor and himself resting on the cot.'

The woman answered smilingly, 'I'm aware that you are fussy and very pugnacious.'

'Pugnacious? Gosh, when did I quarrel with you?'

'Didn't you? Upon that trifle I said to you on the platform, you bullied us with so many words and then you wanted to spend the night in your clerk's house! Now, no more tonight, please go off to sleep like a good boy.'

Next morning, Adharkar woke up at his servant's call, much later than usual. It was almost eight o' clock. He hurriedly changed and found breakfast ready to be served on the table. Responding to his good-morning, the woman smiled, 'Last night you said that you would be deprived of sleep on the cot, thinking of your guests who were sleeping badly on the floor. Your conscience would prick you! Is this your evidence of sleeplessness? Eight o' clock—with your conscience pricking?'

Adharkar replied bashfully, 'I see that my rascal conscience also slept like a log as I fell asleep.'

Laughter rolled on the table, The lilting note of the female voice mingled with the uproarious laughter of the husband and the lord of the house. She said, 'That's why snoring made sleeping impossible in the adjacent room.'

'Snoring? Do I snore? But I never knew about it.'

'There's the fun. The moment you enter the state of knowing, you snore no more.' Again, that combined roll of male and female laughter filled the air.

A little before evening fell, the guests took leave for their relative's house. They made repeated requests to Adharkar to visit them at his convenience. Adharkar was ready to accompany them right away but for the sake of decency he resisted himself.

Adharkar bade them adieu and returned to take his seat in the veranda. He tried to settle his mind in an English romantic novel like he did on other evenings. But his attention wavered from the pages of the book. He often felt beside himself. Each evening he had the habit of going to the Gymkhana Club to play billiards. That evening he felt no urge to go there.

Mrs Sunanda Banerjee and family stayed for ten days in Bombay. Each afternoon, Adharkar went straight from his office to the house of the Banerjees' relative. In a group, they enjoyed outings to a movie, the Apollo port, the Mahalaxmi temple and the Elephanta caves.

The Banerjee couple returned to their resident town, Lahore, after leaving Bombay. Adharkar stayed on in Bombay and re-entered the tedious cycle of his dull, drab and wearisome mode of living. Mornings did not bring him any expectations; evenings did not bring about intimacy with desired ones, nights did not hold any eagerness of waiting for the next dawn to break. The city sans Sunanda held no charm, no taste and no meaning for him anywhere.

But estrangement is not a permanent separation, nor does it mean all is over. Solace for non-seeing was conveyed through letters, non-speaking was substituted by the written word. Sunanda Banerjee wrote, on reaching Lahore,

'Mr Adharkar, You gave shelter to unknown strangers on a helpless night. Offered generous hospitality without reserve, we are thankful for that. I'll ever remember your courtesies.'

Adharkar wrote back,

'With an overnight stay, you have lent honour to a bachelor's den and have paid invincible tribute to the householder. It is I who should convey gratitude. Courtesies are expressed through actions, it's easy; affection enters the mind, it's difficult to achieve. Mrs Banerjee, your kindness defies words.'

The reply came promptly. 'I find that you excel not only as a host but also as a letter writer. Mister, you are not "Charudutt", you are "Charubaak"–refined in words.'

The game of exchanging letters on both sides continued this way. Those letters had more unspoken content than that expressed; their significance outweighed words.

Unthinkable changes occurred in Adharkar's life. So far, he had spent life with books and machines. Passing examination and earning money were the two signposts of his life. He woke up all of a sudden, as though touched by the magic wand that awakens the sleeping princess in fables, to discover his own self for the first time. Not in the corpus of his learnt-by-rote dry knowledge, neither in his large repository of acquired wealth, but in the endless vacuum of his own starved heart.

On a leisurely evening, at a solitary corner of his room, he found delight in mulling over the memory of Sunanda; She haunted his mind when sleep broke off suddenly at the midnight hour's slumbering stillness; at dawn, the face that emerged in his mind was of Sunanda! He marvelled at his pain and pleasure-swathed feelings, how mysterious, how strange, how unspeakable it was!

The more his own heart became exposed to himself, embarrassment and repentance took over. He took to chastening his weak mind. He felt perturbed at the thought of expressing his feelings to Sunanda, off-guard, in a weak moment.

'Would you like some more gin and lime, Minisahib?' Adharkar asked suddenly stopping midway.

My glass was still half-finished. I raised it and said, '*Alamati bistareno*.'

After a few minutes of silence, Adharkar said, 'Naturally you've taken me for a villain.'

I replied, 'You finish your story. I'm a reporter, not a reformer. In my law book there's no provision of redemption or atonement.'

Following a pause, Adharkar picked up the thread of his story.

He had to go to Lahore after three months in connection with his mill's work. Naturally, he accommodated himself in the house of the Banerjees.

Indians serve guests to secure grace for themselves; show hospitality out of courtesy's sake. But guests may be made one's own only through the strength of cordiality. Sunanda had that in abundance. Adharkar's work in Lahore was over in three days. But untying the knot of a lack of work, after several rounds of cancelling and reserving berths, he returned to Bombay twelve days later. But, Adharkar, who went from Bombay and the Adharkar who returned from Lahore, was not the same man. He underwent a sea change in the meantime.

He went to meet a friend the other afternoon, quite a distance away from the city of Lahore. He hoped to be back before evening. But, unable to avoid the sincere request of his friend, he dined there. On his way back, it rained. Moreover, his carriage broke down midway. Both the horse and the seat of the *tonga* by which he was travelling were equally antiquated. One of the wheels of the running *tonga* suddenly fell apart. The passenger was thrown out of the seat on to the muddy road. The winter outpour of rain in the North outdoes the heavy shower of the rainy season. He was completely drenched, standing uncovered in rain for a long time by the desolate wayside, and when he returned to the abode of the Banerjees, it was pre-dawn and the clock had struck four.

A light knock on the door was responded by none other than Sunanda herself.

'Where had you been in this weather? I was dying of anxiety', her voice choked in suppressed weeping. Untamed tears ran down both her cheeks. To control herself, she swiftly slipped into the ante-room.

Mr Banerjee was awakened by the sound of the door opening. He came down the stairs from the first floor and asked, 'What had happened? Where had you been? We've been frightfully worried for you. In an unknown place, in such foul weather… ; Sunanda didn't even go to bed, only walked to and fro on the veranda. Time and again she ran down stairs, thinking odd sounds to be that of a *tonga* stopping!'

Adharkar explained in detail how the carriage broke down and then begged pardon for his inordinate delay. Sunanda came out of the ante-room and solemnly said, 'Would you change your wet clothes? How many inches of the wheel broke, how the horse jumped, all these may be narrated tomorrow morning and it wouldn't spoil the story. Water is still dripping from your head; I guess heroic content would fall short if pneumonia is not contracted!'

It became clear that the admonisher was close by and had heard the details of how the carriage had broken down.

Adharkar tried to go to sleep in his room. He could not get to it. His mind kept moving round a particular orbit like a bumblebee drawn to a blooming lotus bud. What secret mystery of a female heart today suddenly became manifest through the housewife's eager anxiety for her guest's delay, her long and wakeful waiting, her irascible yet sensitive admonishing and above all, tears streaming down her face? Adharkar left his bed and came out into the open.

The night was almost over. The starless sky was overcast and distant rows of trees along the horizon looked hazy in the diluted darkness of dispersing night. Face to face with this solemn and pacified appearance of the earth, waiting for impending dawn, Adharkar felt, for the first time in his life, the divinely blissful touch of his guiding lord on his forehead. With folded hands, he bowed to someone unseen before him. He was only aware of a repeated music of the words 'I'm blessed, I'm blessed', from within his swelling heart and it spread out all over the world and space, reverberating in the chord of the universe as an unstruck sound.

Adharkar stayed in Bombay and Sunanda in Lahore. A distance of thousand miles. But a count of miles does not show distance, indication of nearness is reflected in the heart. With that invisible yet close connection of hearts, these two distantly placed souls continued to remain nearest to each other.

Sunanda once remarked in the course of talking, 'Charu, speaking in English gives me no pleasure. Were I able to speak Marathi, it would've been wonderful.'

Adharkar answered, 'If the mountain won't come to Muhammad, Muhammad must go to the mountain'.

Adharkar performed wonders. He taught himself Bengali in six months; committed to memory Tagore's verses in about a year; finished reading all worthy Bengali literature in a couple of years.

But for a sister, the members of Adharkar's family were all dead. She lived on the Konkan coast with her husband and children. Communication with her was infrequent. So far, Adharkar was a complete man all by himself, like a flower without a stalk. He enjoyed freedom in his work, thought and manner of living. Now that self-controlled way of living saw a change. He wrote letters to Lahore from Bombay, 'Nanda, a servant of this house is asking for three months' leave with pay. Please write if I should allow him.' Or else, 'A house is on sale at a bargain on Walkeshwar Road in Malabar Hills. Do I buy it?' Entrusting his own good and bad and every concern in the hands of a guardian who was not a kin, who stayed far away and was a total stranger only months ago, Adharkar felt at ease with himself. He never knew before that surrendering had so much happiness, dependence was so peaceful.

Fourteen

Adharkar had to go to Europe on business. Banerjee sahib arrived, with spouse in tow, from Lahore, to see him off at Ballard Pier.

Days rolled into months, months added to a year. The seemingly endless hour of estrangement from the beloved also has an end; Adharkar returned after a year to his homeland. He reached Lahore without delay.

It was early December. Awakened from slumber in the train compartment at dawn, Adharkar looked out of the window and was dazzled by the radiance of golden sun-rays in the clear blue sky. Young green sprouts of *sal* plants swayed a little in the air, moistened with dew. A pair of wagtail chicks on telegraph wires waggled their long tails. He was filled with joy for no reason whatsoever.

Arriving at Lahore station in the afternoon, he found that Mr Banerjee was waiting to receive him. At home he was given a letter by an orderly. In that very familiar handwriting, it had words begging his pardon for the absence. She had to go somewhere with another woman on some work; tea was kept ready for him and he should have the tea. She would return before evening.

Not only was there 'arrangements' for tea but also, the bathtub, ready and filled with water; neatly folded clean towels on towel-racks; a new fragrant soap in a soap-case; the bed was freshly made in the bedroom; a beautiful table-lamp and a few recently published English novels on a small tripod by the bedside; even a posy of white oleander, Adharkar's favourite, was kept in a Jaipuri vase.

There was no dearth in hospitality of which a guest might complain. Despite that, why unfounded pensive shadows were cast on his mind's horizon, he could not gather. While abroad, on sleepless nights, time and again, he had so affectionately built up in his mind this very hour. He had spent his leisure hours in working out which words, what news and questions would take precedence among all the accumulated undelivered ones, when they would meet after a gap of twelve months. When would they actually be meeting? All preset and orchestrated plans had been overtaken by a simple question, 'How are you? How have you been?'. Nothing of the sort happened. Adharkar's mind carped. It seemed as though the golden dawn of the dewy season which had brought unbound joy to him didn't meet its match at the end of the day.

Adharkar stayed for a week in Lahore. Although Sunanda's service, care and hospitality had no pitfalls in it, yet the old melody failed to play upon the mind of Adharkar; the guest's heart was not softened. No indication whatsoever could be identified as to where the shortcoming was or what the exceptions had been. Only a pain reigned in the inner chamber of his heart. Is there any means to remove the agony born of want which is not observable in the eyes but is perceptible in the mind?

Had Sunanda changed? No, it is not apparent. Yet, the mind suggests a lack of something. Trifles, the sharpest yet, as little and as unseeable as the budding *kus* grass, pierce Adharkar's sensibility like thorns. But these are so inconsequential that complaining of them would be ridiculous. There is nothing to wonder about if Sunanda fails to note for an entire day that a button is torn in Adharkar's coat. For a housewife who has to bear the entire responsibility of running a big family, it is not unusual. It's logical. But the human mind is not a textbook of inductive logic. It immediately questions, why so now? This has never happened before!

On the day of his departure from Lahore, Adharkar went to bid adieu to friends; they were acquaintances of the Banerjees. Adharkar was endeared to the family on account of Sunanda's friendship with them. The daughter asked, 'What makes you depart as early as today? You came only the other day!'

'Not "only the other day", it's almost ten days now!'

'Ten days? It can't be. I say, it is fewer. Seven days. Well, let's have a bet. You arrived last Saturday; it was the day when Sunanda-di, Ranu-aunty and all of us went to a movie.'

'Went to a movie?'

'Yes, Ranu-aunty visited us that day! Sunanda-di was her classmate at St. Andrew's, you know? She insisted on going to see a movie with her. Tickets were already booked when the news of your arrival reached that afternoon. Sunanda-di wanted to avoid going to the movie because you were coming, but the following morning, Ranu-aunty was to leave Lahore. So, at last, she gave in after much persuasion. You are not listening to me. What are you thinking about? But, you have lost the bet.'

The apparent impression of pain on Adharkar's visage was difficult to assume as appropriate for losing the bet alone. While going back home, he didn't utter a word about it.

To see Adharkar off at the station that evening, husband and wife both accompanied him as usual. At a corner in the waiting room, Sunanda asked, 'You look so unmindful all day today, why? What are you thinking so much about?' Adharkar was startled but checked himself; he merely said, 'Oh, no, not at all.'

The train took off. The waving crowd of well wishers on the platform gradually faded into darkness. The red light of the distant signal also passed beyond sight.

Laying down his tired torso on the berth, Adharkar again reflected on that same theme which had been haunting him since morning. How could Sunanda have preferred the company of her friend over him on the day of his coming? How could a movie outbid the urge of union with the beloved? The tickets were booked? How fabulously costly might that be? Was it only because she had made a promise to a friend? Could nothing change this really? Notwithstanding, Adharkar couldn't think of a situation or an engagement which he might not ignore at perfect ease, solely to welcome Sunanda. Suppose, Sunanda came to Poona from London after a year, or, say from Lahore to Bombay, wouldn't Adharkar set aside his closest friend's pleas on an imaginary pretext of a headache or an illness? Wasn't there a sense of happiness even in lying for the sake of the beloved?

Well, may be it was not possible to pass up the request of an old friend. Compulsion such as tickets bought beforehand stood in the way. There was nothing to blame her for. But, it didn't call for secrecy or fabricating a story.

He spent restless days in Bombay, couldn't stay there for long. He returned to Lahore again. Nevertheless, he failed to bring harmony and rhythm back into his life, it continued like a *khayal* that has lost its tempo midway. As though the edifice built in bits and bobs over three long years on the foundation of two hearts, not bound by ties of kindred, fell off the centre of gravity. Again he returned to Bombay. In this way, he alternated between restless sojourning in Bombay and Lahore.

Finally, the curtain came down on this restless pining very unexpectedly one day.

Moved to agony and apprehension, Adharkar was in Lahore again. Although a basis for grieving overtly was hard to come by, because Adharkar's claim over Sunanda was not one of right, it was of feelings. It was a requisition of the heart. The heart that was often laden with only tears like in an unreasonable child. In the mid-hour on that day, as he was going out to work, Sunanda didn't show up; she didn't hand him his kerchief, fountain pen, wrist watch and purse. The maid informed him, '*Memsaab rasui mein aloo banati hain.*' On his way back from office the following evening, Adharkar spotted none waiting for him on the first floor veranda. He was told that *Memsaab* was busy in matching the list of laundered clothes with the washerwoman.

Nothing had happened to be really offended about. But the emotion-stricken mind indicated that such mishaps had never occurred before. Memsahib's irresistible attachment to slicing potatoes in the pantry or exercising vigilance against the washerwoman's predilection to steal had never been observed before, at the moment of exit or entry of Adharkar.

Mr Banerjee was too occupied in his office and was to return late. In the eve of nightfall, Adharkar proposed, 'Let's go to Sahadara Gardens.'

Sunanda replied, 'No.'

Still, Adharkar insisted that she come.

'What's wrong? Let's go.'

'No, what would people say, seeing me alone with you?'

Adharkar lost his words in wonder. It was not so long ago that one would have to churn memories to remember it. Only before his going to the Continent, they had gone together to Shalimar Gardens, to movies, to the beach in Juhu, to restaurants in Bombay. It was Sunanda who took the initiative to visit the Golden Temple at Amritsar while Mr Banerjee was in Lahore. Where were people then, where was his co-traveller's exceptional regard for their comments?

What would people say?

Alas, once in the past it was Adharkar who had raised this apprehension first.

That year an epidemic of pox broke out in Bombay after the winter was over. Adharkar became infected by it. Somehow, the news arrived in Lahore. The next evening, Sunanda was at Adharkar's flat in Bombay. Adharkar was taken aback, 'You?'

Her reply came in a tone mixed with anxiety, affection and anguish, 'Who else would also suffer? How many days has it been?'

'Four days. I thought not to trouble you with the news.'

'How thoughtful, indeed? Else, how do you propose to kill me off by worries?'

Adharkar was concerned, 'It's contagious. Who advised you to be here?'

Sunanda replied angrily, 'Look, don't make me angry. Who advised me? My fate egged me on.' She asked after a pause, 'Where are your rascal servants and bearers?'

'The cook and the bearer have left in fear. My Madrassi driver is there. He brings me medicines.'

'Excellent arrangement! Only a condolence notice is left to be given out to the newspaper!'. Sunanda went out in search of the driver. She carried her belongings from the taxi upstairs, with his help. Dusted and cleaned the room and made the bed afresh after removing dirty linens. She herself prepared the diet for the patient.

Adharkar asked, 'I don't see Mr Banerjee?'

'He hasn't come.'

'Hasn't come? Who did you come with?'

'I came all alone.'

'What do you mean?'

'Mean what? He is out on tour; will return in about five days. I came across your agent in Lahore in a shop, the day before yesterday, in the morning. I heard of your illness from him. I just managed to lock my house in time to catch the eleven-thirty train, in a mad scramble. I've wired him to come here.'

Overwhelmed in amazement, Adharkar said, 'Won't Banerjee be angry?'

'Maybe he will.'

Remaining silent for a while Adharkar said, 'What will other people say? Why did you not wait till Banerjee's return? Why did you come all alone?'

Sunanda replied, annoyed, 'I've come here because I wanted to. You needn't bother about what people might say. Please go off to sleep in peace.' She moved to the window from the chair by the bedside.

There was not much light within the room. To dim the effect of the light on the patient's eyes, a side of the table lamp was kept covered by the newspaper. Only a part of Sunanda's face was visible from behind. She had taken a bath a while ago. Her dishevelled wet hair spread over her back. She wore a handloom sari. Below her left shoulder, beneath the cover of the curved frills of her sari, elegantly extended her graceful and perfectly round arm. Faintly visible was the glint of a fine gold chain about her raised neck. This silent and dimly lit image of the woman-by-the-window appeared as the quintessence of the most profound assurance to the bed-ridden Adharkar. Neither spoke. Only the deep emotion of the two swelling hearts kindled aloft in an invisible flame above all the mundane trifles and meanness of everyday living, like the hallowed fire in a temple.

Banerjee arrived the next day. Adharkar was diagnosed with chickenpox, not smallpox. As soon as he was healed, Sunanda took him, perforce, to Lahore and he was not permitted to return to Bombay before a fortnight.

Sunanda of that time was not obsessed with outwardly appearances, she didn't care for people's censure, her mind was above the reach of the praise and blame of people around her. She was then not attached to family chores, domestic needs didn't appeal to her, even attention to her husband wavered. Many a day, Adharkar took to reminding Sunanda, 'Banerjee has returned from office. Please go and attend to his needs.'

Sunanda replied, 'Well, well, now I have had it! You'd better not teach me housewifery. It seems as though you are Banerjee's second spouse.'

Sunanda of then was neither a mother, nor a daughter, nor a wife. She was only a paramour. She was not Sunanda Banerjee, she was Sunanda the siren.

She was not a Hindu but a Christian. Many years ago her grandfather had come to settle down in Lahore. Sunanda grew up in a European ambience, was educated in a convent of whites and was married in the Christian manner. In their society, young women did not hide themselves behind the veil; married women were not residents of a *zenana*. Free mixing with men was not reprehensible, moving around with a male friend outside home was not forbidden. Even a divorce followed by a remarriage would not have been taboo in the case of Sunanda.

Adharkar realised in his heart the hard and bitter truth. Sunanda had recovered from infatuation. The ambrosial cup had run out. Churning it any more would only bring out poison instead of nectar.

Adharkar was not eager to return home that afternoon. He telephoned to convey that. He roamed around aimlessly for a considerable time and at last reached the movie theatre at the Mall. Something crossed his mind; he bought a ticket and entered the theatre. The movie had already started. The ticket checker helped him take a seat in the darkness. It was a silent movie. The whirring sound of the running projector was audible. Viewers freely exchanged opinions and chattered along.

Adharkar started, hearing his name. The occupants of the row in front of him were not visible in the darkness, but it was beyond doubt that they were of the fairer sex. Adharkar was all ears to overhear.

'Let go of them all, please don't add to your number of admirers any more. Poor Adharkar was killed by your hand! What more?' said a female voice in a hushed tone.

The reply came promptly, 'Indeed. He confided to you in your ear?'

Adharkar almost fell from his seat. How could he possibly mistake this voice for someone else's? This voice was tied inseparably with the history of his life. He had heard it for the first time three years ago, at Dadar station.

The two friends continued their jests and prattled in a low tone, but not a word escaped Adharkar.

She, who questioned, said, 'Why to my ear alone? Do we not see? It's clear that the gentleman's hope of survival is all lost.'

'Oh, my! How sympathetic! Then, milord, why don't you save him?'

'Oh, really! Would you stand that? Wouldn't that wane the glow of the full moon from my dear friend's face and darken it like the new moon night? I'll have to lose my best friend.'

'Not a bit. I swear I don't give a damn. Rather, I'll feel free if I were rid of him.' Her voice was not diluted by jest.

The questioner perhaps was taken aback by the reply. She avoided making fun and asked reservedly, 'Why dear? Adharkar appears to be a good man. He is gentle, educated and rich but not a snob, rather simple.'

'Not simple, a simpleton. He lacks common sense so much. He takes everything very seriously. Maybe occasionally I've done something or said something for fun sometime but he assumed that I'm in love with him. An idiot! I'm really quite tired, believe me.'

Suddenly the picture was interrupted as the film in the projector snapped; the lights were switched on. In that light, the discussing duo was seen in nearby seats.

In a few minutes, the film was mended and the picture began. The lights were switched off.

The storyline of the movie involved the love affair of the young daughter of a business tycoon. Her destitute lover was about to leave for a far-off country in search of a living. The young lady met him in the garden house in the evening furtively. She insisted on being with him, leaving her father's house. But the young man refused to draw her into poverty. He pleaded, 'You forget me. Take it as though we met unexpectedly in an inn one evening, and at daybreak the next day, all the travellers have gone their different ways and will not meet again.'

The love of the tycoon's daughter was deep. To her, worldly comforts were insignificant, the attraction for riches and wealth had no meaning. The one to whom she had given away her heart, oh how could she live without him? Oh my cruel darling, if you leave your hapless lover behind, trample her lovelorn heart, you may be sure of her death then.

The audience was hooked to the screen with bated breath.

What would the young hero do at the surrender of the lovesick girl? Adharkar would have felt most happy had the hero tightly slapped the profusely powdered cheek of the heroine. But how would it be so? The picture showed a rising full moon in the sky, a clump of flowers on creepers, a pair of curlews on the branch of a tree, making love by pecking each other with their beaks and in the pond in the garden, a pair of full-bloomed lotuses came floating suddenly from two sides, to unite together. The youth acted in the familiar manner resembling Indian movie stars. In this same milieu, he embraced the heroine. They set out together, holding hands. Where to, only the director of the movie knew! The clapping of hands by the enchanted audience filled the auditorium. The drama was over.

Adharkar slipped out of the hall without anyone noticing. He mused that such absurdity was possible only in drama. In drama, there were no compulsions to face real people This gave liberty to the heroine mouthing unnatural words and behaving impossibly. As a mark of relish, we, the spellbound viewers, paid tribute with 'encore, encore'. We did not know that the scenes of the tycoon's daughter expressing love, which filled our eyes with tears, had actually been stage-managed and were pure fun. Sheer hoax. The wretched hero realised it a couple of days after. But the audience had no access to see that. He was always beyond public gaze, out of the composed verses, behind the drama which was staged. Life begins where drama ends!

Adharkar left Lahore that very night.

The train was at twelve midnight. The *tonga* rolled along the stone-paved road slowly. Adharkar had taken this path so many times. But this departure was not like the earlier ones. Departing then bore within it the reassurance of a not-so-distant return, the wistful yearning for reunion. It's all over today. Scarcely any possibility existed to retrace the stretch of the road that fell behind, to pass by the door of the house just crossed.

It is seen in battlefields that after a bomb blast, the severed arm of a wounded soldier lies a short distance away; though he has not lost his senses. While being transported away by an ambulance, the injured man helplessly watches his own torn arm being left behind. Adharkar experienced that same feeling. He perceived through his own eyes as though he was leaving behind his own heart, not an arm, cracked to a hundred smithereens.

It's fun indeed! Not affection, not love, not a trace of breath from the beauty and aroma entwined emotions of the heart, only fun. The remedy of unrequited love is found in compassion, but one who is ridiculed has no solace. His humiliation is unbearable.

Taking as truth the deception of this heartless woman blindly, Adharkar committed a blunder, he developed deep distaste for himself. Remembering how many times he'd unburdened his heart's secrets to her in an inebriated loquacity, how many dreams he had weaved around her, Adharkar repeatedly cursed himself.

Adharkar journeyed back in intense pain and an unbound sense of shame. Millions of stars which keep constant vigil on this wide earth from a zillion miles away in the endless sky, witnessed the unfolding of one more tragedy. For over so many centuries, thousands of such painful heart-rending tragedies have been played out in front of their unwinking, steady eyes, time and again. So many playful acts come to a stop, so many flowers are shed to the ground, so many flutes go silent.

Adharkar had spent almost all his life alone. It was only the other day when he was happy all by himself in his flat, equipped solely with servants and helpers. Now, again, he returned to that lonely solitariness. But the two situations were so radically different. The sky seemed now one big hollow; air carried no meaning, the entire chores and functions of this teeming world tasted dull and wearisome.

Adharkar contemplated about his past, present and future. It appeared to him like a massive, lifeless desert. No trace of a shade anywhere, not a dash of verdant green, not a touch of pleasant interplay of light and shadow.

Adharkar was a fool indeed. He had mistaken a shard of glass for diamond, had misapprehended a bright piece of copper, for a guinea just out of the mint. His attention caught an article written by Gandhiji on modern women. They, Gandhiji wrote, thought themselves a Juliet, the heart-throb of half a dozen Romeos at a time. It appeared to Adharkar that he could get to the meaning of it at last.

But his conviction wavered. He was in a quandary. Could it be possible to spend tense, sleepless nights for several Romeos who were out in foul-weather? Was it possible to negotiate a distance of a thousand miles ignoring family and husband at the news of their illness?

For a few months after his return to Bombay he strived with much vim to dissolve his self completely into work. He laboured hard in the work of the mill from dawn to dusk. He tried to erase the memory of the last three years' short-lived phantasm. He sought to start afresh. But the human mind is not the slate of children which can be wiped clean at will to begin writing afresh. Battling day in and day out with himself, Adharkar became thoroughly bruised in mind and spirit. Then, one day, he sold his mill at dirt cheap rates and vanished from Bombay.

He went to Malaya and became a manager at a rubber plantation. He didn't like it there for long. He left for Ceylon as the head of a coffee company but couldn't stay there for even two years.

He worked at a wine distillery in Buenos Aires; felt disgusted there too. He roamed around many countries as a traveller for a long time. Nanking, Canberra, Toronto, Washington, Leipzig, Brussels. Yet his mind was not settled.

Adharkar had once purchased a few machines for his mill from an English company in Newcastle. He came to Delhi at last as the manager of that company's India operations. He has been serving this company for almost eleven years now. The managing director of the mill which he had sold twenty years ago is a multi-millionaire now. In that mill, today, serve a dozen employees whose salaries are more than that of Adharkar.

Year after year elapsed. Adharkar has reached the sunset hour of his life now. Signs of ageing are becoming more and more manifest on him. The severe intensity of heartfelt emotions, peculiar to a younger age, is now dimmed in strength.

Sunanda of Adharkar's love was not only the flesh and blood bound part of her being. Love, according to its depth, reflexively inducts within itself a mesh of illusions. By dint of that illusion, we fabricate our beloved after our liking in our minds. We assign that beauty to her which she does not possess. We assume on her that quality which she lacks. She is not a creation of god; she is a new product of the figment of our imagination. So, for the sake of dim-looking girls when good-looking, rich youths forsake everything, other people wonder, 'What does she have, what in her has bewitched him?' What actually bewitched him was not in her possession, it's in the mind of the entranced lover's creative imagination, in the vision of his eyes smitten by love. He composed her image in radiant hues of elegance and allure of his own creation.

The vision in Adharkar's eyes are no more smitten by love; the mesh of illusion is also removed from his mind. The image of Sunanda which he had once composed, bit by bit, amassing all the charm and range of colourful imaginations of all the poets of the world, is today disposed off in the limbo of oblivion. For him, Sunanda is now reduced to an utterly insignificant woman. Nowhere about her remains a vestige of that exquisite exclusivity which once adorned her.

What a mystery is the human mind! Even today, the root of the wound exists deep inside him, although the scar has disappeared. Why does it still smart if touched in an unguarded moment? Why does memory never fade out?

Adharkar's story ended.

We sat in inarticulate silence for some time.

'*Huzur*, may I get you a *tonga*?'

I was startled and found Adharkar's servant standing nearby. I didn't quite notice when Adharkar had silently risen and left. He had just made a disclosure of his life's profound secret to a recently acquainted friend of a dissimilar age. When he went on with the telling of the story, he bathed in the flow of his memories. As soon as the story was over, the trance was broken; he landed in the real world of direct experiences. He felt awkward the moment we exchanged looks. So he reticently disappeared. I desisted myself from seeking his permission to go. I told the servant not to and moved out into the street.

The gibbous moon shone brightly in the cloudless sky and spread its light over wide courtyards of the bungalows on either side of the road. The road ahead was empty and quiet. Hasnahana shrubs had flowered somewhere near by. Redolent with its intensely besotting fragrance, the night had become as though dazed and the air, thick in ardent fervour.

I was thinking of Adharkar as I walked along the road. His confessions played out in my ear, 'Minisahib, I'm an idiot indeed! I took frolicking for love; regarded playfulness as truth. But I'm not alone. It is my kind of idiots in this world that have made life so full of variety; a kaleidoscopic variety of weal and woe. For ages this foolish hapless lot made mistakes, fell in love, then cried for the rest of their lives. Tears that wrung out of their hearts have made the everyday life in this world flavoured and charming. Their mistakes, shortcomings, idiocies have been the subject of verses for poets, theme of songs for ascetics, a model for artists and for sculptors to carve out wonderful beauty in stone. Intelligent people of the world will make a career in service, get married, save money in banks, order ornaments from jewellers; will lead a trouble-free life of affluence, with their husbands or wives, sons and daughters. Nonetheless, we the band of nitwits will never accept that only those who deceived, made fun of love, gave chalk water for milk, are the winners in this world and losers are those who gave love in exchange of jest.'

Too weak a consolation indeed! It's easy to quote Tagore, 'Whatever life's riches are will not go unutilised, even if it lies ignored in dust.' But life is not only a sheer string of arguments without human touch. Poetic metre may be created by garlanding words, but real life can't be led that way.

Adharkar belongs to that class of men who can't keep anything in hand. These people are destined to suffer. Like in politics, human life is also about adjustment and compromise. Even in these days of rocketing inflation, only the value of the heart is not much in our day to day life.

It was not possible for Sunanda to move in pace with Adharkar. She was a woman. Love was only a commonplace event for her. It is not a discovery, as it is to men. Girls are naturally always on their guard and so they fall in love to build nests. Love is a mere necessity for women, it is as ordinary as the daily wear of women attending to humdrum household chores; this has neither cheer, nor wonder, nor ebullience. For men, love is life's rare luxury, it's as opulent as a Benarasi silk sari in a poor man's hut; he who has it, achieves it for a high price. So, it's only men who, for love's sake, may forsake things which are ordinarily difficult to get and may make things possible, which are otherwise impossible to achieve.

Adharkar himself said one day, 'Minisahib, in this world, only King Edwards have abdicated thrones for Mrs Simpsons. Instances are aplenty across time and space of men leading their whole life on their own as a token of their love for a married woman; no woman ever remained a spinster for the cause of loving a married man.'

I'm not known for my soft-heartedness. But I truly felt pangs in my heart for Adharkar. I've no idea of the present whereabouts of Sunanda Banerjee. It can be inferred that passing years have taken away her youth, her over-the-hill physique has lost its charm, her looks are no more electrifying and the wrinkles on her forehead are defying all attempts to remain hidden under the cover of cosmetics. No means are available to know if in any unhurried moment, ever, her mind unsettles for a while remembering the utter foolishness displayed long ago by a Marathi Brahmin. Curiously, it's for her alone that Adharkar paid the ultimate price. He deprived himself of success, of fame, of all worldly happiness. Above all, he deprived himself of a possible successor and let his lineage go extinct.

No one would ever light an earthen lamp at nightfall before the holy basil sanctum, praying for his good, no woman will ever wear vermilion in the parting of her hair, desiring his welfare and long life; no mind will ever be anxious and listless with unbearable aching for not seeing him long. When in bed and ill, no worry-stricken palm will lend a comforting touch to his forehead, no distressed teardrop will roll down anyone's cheek. On the day he will cease to exist, no rent heart will ache a whit, no mind will preserve the faintest memory.

Love gives glory to life, conveys dignity to death. But what does it bestow to the deceived? It chars. The fire which does not illumine but only sears, that lack-lustre fire, by and by, has mercilessly burnt the ingenuous and hapless Charudutt Adharkar.

A reckoner for the readers

1. 23 March 1942
2. Canadian quintuplets, b. 28 May 1934, to Elzire, wife of Olive Dionne, of Callander, Ontario
3. 12 April 1942

The Book

- First printed in book form between September and October 1947; was presented with the Narasimha Das Award by Delhi University in 1950
- The Hindi translation by Namita Lumba was published in 1960
- A dramatised version by the author was aired by All India Radio, Calcutta, in March 1949

Milestones

- Willingdon airport is now Safdarjang airport, Queensway is now Janpath, Kingsway and Yorkplace are now Rajpath and Motilal Nehru Place respectively
- Departments of the British era are now Ministries; Home Ministry has shifted to North Block from South Block in 1967-68
- BBCI Railway is now a part of Western Railway
- Swiss Hotel has been replaced by Oberoi Apartments
- Queen Victoria Road is now Dr Rajendra Prasad Road; the bungalow no. 3 on the road is no longer there; Shastri Bhavan has taken its place
- The row of six similar bungalows on King Edward Road and Queen Victoria Road (renamed later after Independence as the Maulana Azad Road and Dr Rajendra Prasad Road respectively) has been replaced by new constructions, Nirman Bhavan and Vijnan Bhavan
- Reading Road is now Mandir Marg (a name very close to 'Temple Street' indeed!)
- In the central government, Superintendent is now Section Officer; Assistant Secretary ceases to exist; now, the person above the Section Officer is Under Secretary
- Imperial Delhi Gymkhana is now only Delhi Gymkhana